THE
NOEL
LETTERS

RICHARD PAUL EVANS

THE
NOEL
LETTERS

FROM THE NOEL COLLECTION

GALLERY BOOKS

NEW YORK   LONDON   TORONTO   SYDNEY   NEW DELHI

Gallery Books
An Imprint of Simon & Schuster, Inc.
1230 Avenue of the Americas
New York, NY 10020

First Gallery Books hardcover edition October 2020

GALLERY BOOKS and colophon are registered trademarks of Simon & Schuster, Inc.

For information about special discounts for bulk purchases, please contact Simon & Schuster Special Sales at 1-866-506-1949 or business@simonandschuster.com.

The Simon & Schuster Speakers Bureau can bring authors to your live event. For more information or to book an event, contact the Simon & Schuster Speakers Bureau at 1-866-248-3049 or visit our website at www.simonspeakers.com.

Interior design by Erika R. Genova

Manufactured in the United States of America

1 3 5 7 9 10 8 6 4 2

Library of Congress Control Number: 2020942029

ISBN 978-1-9821-2960-6
ISBN 978-1-9821-2961-3 (ebook)

In memory of Carolyn Reidy

THE
NOEL
LETTERS

P R O L O G U E

When I was young, my father taught me some-thing that has given me considerable insight into humanity: *As you walk through life*, he said, *don't be surprised to find that there are fewer people seeking truth than those seeking confirmation of what they already believe.*

My father was right. I'm amazed at the mental gymnastics we go through to protect our beliefs—even when they're our own worst enemy. Sometimes it seems the shakier the belief, the tighter our grip.

I'm not judging humanity as much as I'm judging myself, as that perfectly described me when this story took place. This is a story about the lies I nurtured and what happened when they were exposed to truth. You could say this is the story of my awakening.

I was born with the last name of Book. Maybe that's why I became a writer. I know that sounds like a joke but it's not. Research has proven that your name influences what you'll do in life. For instance, there's a statistically improb-able number of men named Dennis who become dentists. And people with the last name Cook are 20 percent more likely to pursue a career in the culinary arts. It's true; look it up.

It's certainly true in my experience. My father, Robert Book, owned a bookstore. And here I am, writing a book.

My full name is Noel Book, which sounds like either the name of a holiday-themed bookstore or the publisher of Christmas tales, which, ironically, isn't far from the truth. When this story began, I was working in New York as an editor for one of the Big Five publishers. I've worked on more than my fair share of holiday books.

Actually, the surname *Book* has nothing to do with literature. It's of Scottish origin and refers to a region in Scotland called Boak, which, regrettably, means "to belch" or " to nearly throw up." It's not exactly the kind of name that strikes fear in the hearts of your enemies. Growing up I was teased for my last name. I'm just grateful no one ever found out its true meaning. I had few enough friends as it was.

Adding to my overall ostracization by my peers was the fact that my vocabulary was advanced for my age. My father was to blame for that. He spoke like a dictionary. He didn't do it to impress, the way some people do; it was just the way he talked. It was as if he had a license to use more words than most. Sometimes it sounded like a different language. One time he told a man off and the guy thanked him. My father liked words and he was smart, which, I guess, rubbed off on me.

When I was eight years old he would quiz me on the *Reader's Digest* Word Power section. I just thought it was something all parents did with their kids. The result was that I spoke like my teachers, which, of course, the other kids teased me about. In middle school a boy called me Thesaurus

Rex—a name that both hurt and stuck. It was the same year my mother was killed in a car accident, the first falling domino that set off the entire awful chain of events that became my life.

That was the same year I stopped dancing. It was also the year that the fissure opened between me and my father. There's no doubt the two were connected. My father loved to watch me dance, and I had stopped loving my father.

For almost two decades I nurtured the distance between my father and me. Then, in one holiday season that changed. It was the time that the letters arrived.

If you choose to read my story, I ask just one mercy. I'm not proud of who I was back then. Please don't judge me too harshly or too quickly. I've already done that for you. And my sins carry their own punishment. Thankfully, there are still a few people out there who aren't afraid of truth. And there are still a few people who know how to love—even someone as unlovable as me.

CHAPTER

one

I can stand about anything for a week if I have a good enough book.

—Noel Book

"Is Salt Lake City home for you?"

I looked over at the smiling, silver-haired woman sitting inches from me in the middle seat of our row. On her lap were two knitting needles impaling the rectangular mass of what looked like a blanket. She had smiled at me as we boarded the plane at JFK, but she had sat knitting so quietly throughout the flight I'd forgotten she was even there. Or maybe I'd just been too preoccupied winding my way through the labyrinth of my thoughts. At any rate, her question vexed me. I wasn't sure where home was anymore. I wasn't even sure if I knew what the word meant.

"I was born there," I said softly. "But I haven't been back for sixteen years."

"Goodness, that's a long time to be away. What brings you back now?"

"I'm going to see my father."

Her smile broadened. "I've always loved a homecoming. After all that time, you must be so excited to see him."

"He's dying," I said.

Her expression fell. "I'm sorry, dear. God bless you."

"Thank you." I looked back out the window at the snow-covered world below. The crystalline blanket reflected the light of the winter moon in a dull cobalt blue. The Wasatch Range was taller than I remembered, rising in a jagged ridge running in a near-perfect line north to south of the valley like a great snow wall. The buildings below looked small and flat and well-spaced, nothing like New York, where every street was a slot canyon and every building a mountain.

Home. Homeward bound. One of my colleagues at the publishing house called me a hobo, which she said was a contraction of "homeward bound." Of course, I looked it up. Maybe. Or it might be a contraction of "homeless boy," or even a derivative of Hoboken, New Jersey. It's another one of those words that slipped into the back row of our cultural lexicon without a ticket.

My anxiety rose with each passing minute. I hadn't even taken the book I'd brought with me out of my carry-on, which pretty much shows the state I was in. After all this time, I had no idea what I would say to my father. Actually, I was more concerned about what he would say to me. Maybe it would be a weeklong shame festival with a dying man. *Why was I doing this?* I think if I could have turned the plane around I probably would.

The previous holiday, a colleague told me she was going home for Thanksgiving for the first time in five years. She had hopes for reconciliation with her mother. Her anticipated home-coming lasted less than an hour. She likened the experience to an emotional ambush. Seven hours later she was back in New York eating a Banquet turkey potpie for Thanksgiving. The difference between her experience and mine is that I had no such expectations. My father was dying. The most I could hope for was to put the past in a box and bury it. Literally as well as figuratively.

When my father was first diagnosed with cancer, the doctor had given him six months to live, which he hadn't told me until the last two weeks when, I guess, he finally accepted that he was engaged in a losing battle. That's when he asked to see me one last time. *There are things that need to be said.* Those words scared me most of all.

He had invited me to stay at his house, my childhood home, adding that my room was exactly the same as I'd left it almost two decades ago. I had resisted the invitation, it was my MO, but he was anticipating my rejection. "Noel," he said softly. "It's our last chance."

What could I say to that? Frankly, I didn't need the expense of a hotel. New York is expensive and book editors aren't exactly overpaid. He had also offered to pay for my flight and the use of his car, which he obviously wouldn't be using while I was there. From the sound of things, probably never again.

I consoled myself that it would only be a week. I could stand anything for a week.

My father had arranged for Wendy, the manager of his bookstore, to pick me up from the airport. I had met her, but it had been a while. We were roughly the same age, though she always seemed like a much older soul to me. She'd started working part-time at the bookstore just a few months before I left, and had worked her way up to manager. I remembered that she was pretty, in a different sort of way. She had the slight, lanky figure of a Lladró statuette, with bright carrot-colored hair and a matching complexion. The thing I remembered most about her was that she worshipped my father. Even back then I thought of her as obsequious—lapping up every word my father said as though he were Plato. She was Team Robert. I wasn't. I wondered if there would be tension.

Typical for the holidays and New York, it was an over-crowded flight, and when the plane's seatbelt bell chimed, most of the passengers jumped from their seats as if they were spring-loaded. I didn't. I was in no hurry to deplane. I'd checked two pieces of luggage and I'd rather sit alone on the plane than make awkward conversation with someone I barely knew and assumed didn't like me.

I also wasn't in a hurry to see my father—not just to see him in his compromised condition but to confront my absence from his life. It was like ignoring someone's phone call for a week then running into them at the mall. Except a thousand times that. *Things that need to be said.*

"Good luck, dear," the old woman said to me as she rose from her seat, her bag of yarn and needles tucked away in the vinyl Trader Joe's grocery bag hanging from her shoulder.

It was nearly ten minutes later that the plane had fully emptied. I retrieved my carry-on from the overhead bin and left the plane as the flight attendants made their sweep of the aircraft.

It had been quite a while since I'd been in the Salt Lake airport. The last time I was there was especially memorable. Someone had stolen my laptop when I'd set it down in a bookstore to look for one of my authors' books. I was changing planes on a layover to Los Angeles and never even left the terminal. My ex-husband, Marc, never let me live that down.

I stopped at the Starbucks near the security exit and got myself a Venti latte and finished it before heading down to claim my luggage. As I came down the escalator, Wendy was waiting for me in a stanchioned waiting area holding a piece of paper with my name on it. I was a little surprised that I recognized her so quickly, even though she was hard to miss. She was wearing a bright orange ski parka—which only drew more attention to her ginger complexion—black leggings, and fur-lined boots. A small purse hung over her arm. She was prettier than I remembered. Striking, even.

I stepped off the crowded escalator and walked in her direction. She recognized me as well, lowering her sign and stepping toward me. As I neared, I noticed her eyes were red and swollen.

When we were close, she said, "Hi, Noel, I'm Wendy."

"I remember you," I said.

"It's been a few years," she said softly. She looked at me with dark eyes. "Your father passed away four hours ago."

I didn't know what to say. I wasn't even sure what I felt.

"I'm sorry," she said. She breathed out slowly, took her hand from her coat pocket, and wiped her eyes with a Kleenex. After another long moment she looked down at my carry-on and said, "Do you have more luggage?"

"I have two bags."

"Your luggage is on carousel eight. It's this way." She started off toward the west end of the terminal. I followed her, pulling my carry-on behind me. The carousel was already half-full of baggage, and Wendy and I stood next to each other watching the bags come out.

After a few minutes Wendy said, "Do you know how long you'll be staying in Utah?"

"Not long," I said.

I had planned to stay until my father's death. Now that my plan had been upended, I really had no idea how long I was staying. As short as possible. There were too many hard memories. Too much pain.

It was another ten minutes before my luggage emerged. My bags were large, both of them "big enough to hold a body," the guy at the Costco cash register had said. Still, I had to sit on them to zip them shut. My mind said it was a quick stop, but I'd packed like I'd be here for weeks. I'm sure my therapist would have fun with that.

I wrestled my first bag off the carousel as my second bag appeared.

"That ugly purple-burgundy one is mine too," I said to Wendy as the bag passed me. Wendy stepped forward to grab it, though I wasn't sure how she was going to get it down as it was even larger than the first and was riding near the top of the over-crowded carousel. A tall, bearded man wearing a ski patrol parka stepped up and pulled it off, setting it on the ground next to her.

"Thank you," Wendy said. "That was kind of you."

"My pleasure," he said, his smile visible beneath his facial bush. I'm sure Wendy got a lot of that.

Wendy seemed oblivious to it. Or maybe she was just jaded. "You said two bags?"

"This is it," I said.

Wendy pulled the handle up on the suitcase. "All right. Let's go."

We took the elevator up to the skybridge then exited to the

short-term parking garage. The night air was sharp and cold, freezing my breath in front of me in white puffs.

"My car's over there," Wendy said, pointing to an older white Subaru wagon. When we reached it, she lifted the hatch and we put my bags in, which filled the entire back of the wagon.

She unlocked the doors and we simultaneously climbed in. There was cat hair on my seat and footwell. Actually, it was everywhere. Wendy had two Siamese cats: Jennifur and Clawdia. My father had referenced them from time to time. He was allergic to cats. So was I. My eyes watered.

As I put on my seat belt I glanced over at Wendy. Her eyes were closed tight but tears still managed to escape her eyelids and roll down her cheeks.

"Are you okay?"

She didn't answer, but again wiped her eyes. Then she breathed out, leaned forward, and started the car. Christmas music came on. Perry Como, something I was familiar with, as our family listened to it when I was young.

"They're playing Christmas music early here," I said. "In New York the stations don't play Christmas music until after Halloween."

"It's a CD. It makes me happy," she said, then added, "I need a little happy right now." She reached down and turned off the music then turned up the heat. The warm air blew loudly from the dash vents. "Let me know if it gets too hot."

"Thank you."

We drove out of the parking garage then south toward the eastbound I-80 freeway. The Salt Lake airport is only six miles west of the city in what is likely the most desolate part of the valley, the land surrounding the Great Salt Lake.

The only thing that's *great* about the lake, other than its name, is its size. Lakes are usually beautiful places that draw people. The Great Salt Lake did the opposite. Think of it as a North American version of Israel's Dead Sea and you'll understand its lack of appeal.

My parents first took me to the lake as a child. I remembered thinking how pretty it was, its salt crystals sparkling in the sun. My delight vanished the moment I got in and discovered how uncomfortable the saline-rich water felt on my skin. Parts of the Great Salt Lake are ten times saltier than the ocean, which means little can live in it, outside of nasty microbes and the brine shrimp that feed off them. One of the by-products of the salt is hydrogen sulfide, which smells like rotten eggs. Not exactly Lake Tahoe.

Neither of us said much on the ride to my father's house. I just silently looked out the window at the transformed scenery. The city had changed as much as I had since I left. In one of his letters my father had told me that Downtown had doubled in size, which was impressive, but still left it a dwarfed, meager percentile of the Manhattan skyline.

We took Interstate 80 to 215 South, then the ramp east to the Highland Drive exit.

As we pulled into my old neighborhood, the only thing I recognized was the 7-Eleven my father used to take me to every Sunday to buy me a Slurpee and a box of Lemonhead candy. What had been a Taco Bell on the corner was now a dental office—a peculiar and disappointing conversion.

In my eighteen-year absence the trees and bushes had grown, and the aged houses seemed to have shrunk. The street was beautifully tree lined. The area had gentrified as the older residents passed on and younger homeowners moved in, remodeling or outright demolishing the older homes.

The area of the city I'd grown up in was called Sugar House, or Sugarhouse as the locals wrote it. It was named for a sugar beet test factory that had resided there more than a century prior. Sugarhouse was one of Salt Lake's oldest neighborhoods and the tiny home where I'd spent my childhood had been built before World War II on what had once been the Mormon prophet Brigham Young's apricot orchard. One of the few original trees still existed in our yard. The tree produced copious amounts of fruit each year, and I remember watching my mom and dad pick the apricots and place them in baskets, which I'd sell by the side of the road for two dollars a bushel.

The backyard had been magical to me—my own fantastical kingdom where I battled bad guys and villains and ruled with a broom sword. Our backyard neighbor, an elderly woman I called Mrs. Betty, had two frenetic, cotton-white toy poodles that would stick their noses through the space between the fence slats and lick my hand, which delighted me to no end.

The dogs' yapping would alert Mrs. Betty to my presence in the backyard, and I'd hear her slide open her back door and then push her walker through the grass to see me. Looking back, I think she must have been terribly lonesome. Sometimes she would bring me cookies, which tasted of rancid butter but were still sweet and welcomed.

The lady sitting next to me on the plane reminded me of her. I thought about what she had said to me about homecomings. I once edited a book by an author who had fought in the infantry during the Vietnam War. The book shared his emotional journey of going back to see the places where he had served. There was now a McDonald's where there had been an intense firefight and he'd lost his leg and two of his best friends. I remember how his book made me feel. In some ways I felt the same anxious anticipation as Wendy slowly drove down my childhood street.

The house's lights were off, leaving the home dark and still as if it had died along with my father. The yard's only illumination came from the fingernail October moon and the vintage-style streetlamp that straddled the property line between my father's home and the ivy-covered brick house to the south. In the dim light I could see that someone had already left a vase of flowers at the front door.

Wendy pulled into the driveway, put the car in park, and shut off the engine. The quiet of the moment struck me. Not just between us, but the whole new world. Downtown New York is never really quiet, something you sometimes forget until you're away from it.

I suddenly wondered whether my father's body was still inside. *They wouldn't have left it for me, would they?* It was as if Wendy had read my mind. "He's gone," she said, adding, "the funeral home picked him up."

I turned to her. "Was anyone with him when he died?"

"I was. And a nurse from hospice. He was in a lot of pain, so we had him on a morphine drip." I could see tears again welling up in her eyes and, still looking away from me, she furtively brushed a tear from her cheek.

"I'll get my luggage," I said.

Wendy opened the hatch while I walked around and pulled out both bags and my carry-on. Wendy got out of the car and walked to the house's side door and unlocked it using a key from her key chain. She propped open the door, then went to get the one suitcase I had left.

Passing over the threshold was like entering a time machine. I flipped on the kitchen lights then stepped up into the kitchen.

The first thing I noticed was the movement of the Black Forest cuckoo clock on the wall next to the refrigerator, its carved-wood pendulum swinging from side to side above the brass pinecone-shaped counterweights. The clock had transfixed me as a child. My father had brought it back from Germany, and it was unlike any other cuckoo clock I'd ever seen. It had three blue butterflies on its face that moved along with the rest of the clock's mechanics. For the longest time I thought the butterflies were real. It was a constant in the magical thinking of my childhood.

Butterflies were a theme around our house. My father collected butterflies the way some people collect thimbles and little souvenir spoons. He gathered them in different varieties all around the house, from carved olive wood to plastic ornaments. When I was little, he told me they were "flying flowers" that had set themselves free from the constraints and stems of life. I believed him. I used to believe everything he said.

The house smelled antiseptic and dank, like a nursing home or some other place with sick people.

Wendy followed a little way behind me as I walked through the house. I passed through the kitchen to the small dining nook on the southwest corner of the house. There were the same oak table and chairs I had sat at with my cereal or Malt-O-Meal every day before school.

In one corner of the room was a glass menagerie case with

porcelain figurines—soft-curved German Hummels and the larger, glossy Lladró pieces. Most of the sculptures were of butterflies or little statues of girls with butterflies. I remembered most of them from my childhood—especially one of a father holding his daughter's hand. As I looked them over, there was only one I didn't remember. It was a statue of a veiled bride holding a bouquet of roses. It seemed a little out of place in the collection. I wondered when he had purchased it.

I moved from the dining area to the front room. There were two couches in front of a tiled fireplace with a painted mantel and bronze lion-head andirons. There was a large framed picture of me above the fireplace. It was a picture I'd never seen before.

As I stood there, I remembered the flowers someone had left outside on the front porch. I went to get them and suddenly froze. Standing near the front door, I had a flashback of my father holding my mother down as she screamed for him to let her go. My heart started pounding heavily. That experience was indelibly branded on my mind and soul. It was the last time I saw my mother alive.

I fled the discomfort of the living room, down the short hallway that led to the bedrooms. I looked in the bathroom. The old tulip and windmill wallpaper had been stripped and painted over in a neutral taupe. The original black-and-white honeycomb floor tile remained. When I was seven years old I was fascinated by how much the tile looked like chicken coop wire, and one morning I began tracing between the lines with a Magic Marker, an act that earned me a rare spanking from my mother and a lengthy time-out.

The room next to the bathroom had been my parents'.

The door was shut, which is how I remembered it. It was the home's inner sanctum and I rarely went inside. I grasped the brass handle and opened the door. I was hit by a rush of cold air. The room was freezing.

"Why is it so cold in here?" I asked Wendy.

"I cracked the windows to air out the room," she answered. "It smelled bad."

I stepped farther inside. "This is where . . ." I didn't finish.

After a moment she said, "I stripped the sheets and washed them. They're in the dryer."

"Thank you."

"You're welcome."

Wendy walked past me and shut the window on the far side of the room. On top of a mahogany chest of drawers was another Lladró, one of a young girl holding a bouquet of butterflies. It was next to a postcard-sized, silver-framed photograph with the word *Yellowstone*. The picture was of my father and me in front of Old Faithful. I was probably four years old at the time, and I was sitting on his shoulders watching the spout. The picture, the closeness, felt foreign to me.

I took a deep breath and turned back. I'd seen enough. I walked out of the room and across the hall to my old bedroom. I opened the door and flipped on the light. The light switch was still encased in a whimsical, nursery-tale plate that had somehow survived my childhood: Mary and her little lamb.

My room was, as my father said, exactly as I'd left it. The memories were thickest here.

The bed was a wooden poster bed with a princess canopy. As a thirteen-year-old, I had crawled under the bed on that horrible night my mother had fled our house. I woke later in my bed, to tense, emotional voices. For reasons I couldn't fathom, my father's sister was there. She was talking in low tones with my father, who then left the house. I remember hearing the side door slam and the angry roar of the car engine as he drove away. Most of all, I remember the overwhelming fear I felt as I wondered if he or my mother would ever come back.

I woke the next morning and jumped out of bed to see if my parents were there. All I found was my aunt sitting at the kitchen table drinking coffee. She looked as solemn and gray as I felt.

"Where's my dad?" I asked.

"He's still sleeping, honey," she said. Her eyes were puffy and bloodshot, as if she'd cried all night.

"I'm here," my father said, walking in behind me. He looked worse than my aunt. He said to me, "Noel, I need to tell you something." He exhaled slowly, then said, "Come to my room."

I followed him into his bedroom, wondering where my mother was. We both sat on the side of the unmade bed, my feet dangling above the floor. I remember watching him, his eyes welling with tears, wondering what awful thing would come from his mouth. It was worse than I'd imagined. Worse, maybe, than I could have imagined. The nightmare I hoped was ending had only begun. My mother, he told me, was dead. Nothing would ever be the same.

My dresser, which was glossy white like my bed, was covered with photographs of me, most of them taken when I was younger. My father was a shutterbug back when people still took pictures with cameras. Most of the photos were of me dancing; I could trace the evolution of the costumes through the years, from a feathery yellow duck costume in my first dance class to a pink tutu and ballet slippers in my early teens. In one of the pictures I was wearing a middle school cap and gown with a gold honor-student stole.

I walked over to the closet and opened it. My high school clothes were still there. Even the stole was there. I once read that in Victorian etiquette, if a child were to die, the parents would persist with the daily routines of life as if the child were still there—even setting a plate at the dinner table for the deceased. That's what my return felt like. My room was a mausoleum, a holding place for the dead remnants of my childhood and the beginning of the end of my family. The death of a home. I stepped out of the room, turning the light out as I went.

I found Wendy in the kitchen. She was crying again. When she could speak, she said, "He tried to hold on for you. His last words were 'Tell Noel I'm sorry.'"

"Sorry for what?"

"Not being here for you."

I leaned against the sink. "I never thought I'd make it back here."

"Neither did your father." At this the tone of her voice changed. "But he hoped. He always hoped." She sighed loudly. "The man had a lot of misplaced hope."

I couldn't tell from her comment whether she was trying to shame me. There was a distance to her, but maybe it was just grief. She had just lost the person she'd spent more time with than anyone else. Someone she clearly cared about. In a way, the bookstore was their home.

"What will you do with the bookstore?" I asked Wendy.

"I'll keep things running," she said softly. "That's what your father asked me to do until you decided what you wanted to do with it."

I looked at her quizzically. "What *I* want to do with it?"

"I presume he meant he was leaving the bookstore to you."

This was something I'd never considered. "He should have given it to you."

"Blood is thicker than water."

"Not always," I said.

She frowned. "I'm going to go. I've got inventory in the morning."

"You're going in to work?"

"There's a lot to be done."

Her loyalty amazed me. "Thank you for picking me up tonight."

"You're welcome." She paused slowly and looked around the room. There was something melancholy about her gaze, as if she were anticipating that she would never see this house again. I supposed there was a good chance she wouldn't. Her gaze fell back on me. "Your father's keys are in the drawer next to the re-frigerator. The car keys, house keys, the back shed, everything."

I wondered how she knew all this. "Thank you."

"Also, I wrote down the Wi-Fi password. It's that folded paper on top of the fridge."

"Thank you," I said again.

She turned and walked out. A minute after she left, her car still hadn't started. I looked out the kitchen window to see her leaning against her steering wheel. It had started snowing, and thick flakes collected on her car. It was several more minutes before she started the engine, turned on the wipers, and backed out of the driveway. *Welcome home.*

I was startled by the cuckoo clock as it suddenly erupted in a fury of activity, the small cuckoo chirping twelve times while the butterflies' wings flapped in unison.

"Hello, little bird," I said. We had history, that bird and me. I used to stand beneath the clock and wait for its appearance.

Across from me was a framed quote on the wall:

> Enjoy the little things in life
> for one day you'll look back and
> realize they were the big things.
> —*Kurt Vonnegut*

My father collected quotes, and he especially loved those from Vonnegut. I think his favorite Vonnegut quote was

> To be is to do—Socrates
> To do is to be—Sartre
> Do Be Do Be Do—Sinatra

It was as if all the emotions I'd run from hadn't really died but had existed in this timeless place, clinging to the joists and drywall, waiting for my return to resurface.

I went to my bedroom, lay back on the bed, and cried.

That night I had a dream. My father was standing by the side of my bed with my mother. They just stood there silently, holding hands, looking at me.

CHAPTER

two

Take a good book to bed with you—books do not snore.

—Thea Dorn

WEDNESDAY, OCTOBER 28, 2015

I woke to the incessant clucking of the cuckoo. The room's blinds were closed and were glowing against an already high sun. I leaned over and grabbed my phone from the nightstand to check the time. I had forgotten to charge it. It was dead.

I pulled back the sheets, got the charger from my backpack, and plugged in my phone, then went to the kitchen, looking up at the now-silent clock. It was noon. I'd slept for almost twelve hours.

I opened the cupboard where my father had once kept the coffee. I wasn't surprised that it was there. My father was a man of habit. The location was the same, but his taste in coffee had changed. Like most Americans, he had gone from the ubiquitous grocery store brand to a more exotic blend—Kona Vanilla Macadamia Nut.

As I put the coffee on to brew, I heard my phone beep. I walked back to my room to see who had called. I had two text messages and four missed calls, two of them from local numbers I didn't know. There were three voice mails. The first text was from Jerica Bradley, one of my more popular authors. It simply said:

What did you think of revision?? Tossed the LI

LI. Jerica's abbreviation for "love interest." *Haven't read it yet,* I thought. *Some of us need sleep.*

The other text was from a number with an 801 area code, but there was no name attached.

Your father's funeral will be this Saturday. I left you a phone message.

I went to my voice mail. The first message was from my roommate, Diana.

"Hey, Noel, it's Diana. Hope your father is okay. Sorry to bother you during this, but Darrin is moving back in next Wednesday, so I've got to get your things out. When will you be back?"

I groaned and went to the next voice mail.

"Noel, this is Wendy. Your father's funeral will be this Saturday at the church on Parleys Way or Boulevard, whatever they call it. It's the one by the house.

"The viewing starts at nine a.m. and the funeral begins at eleven. I'll have a place saved for you at the front of the chapel. Your father had his funeral planned out. He didn't put you on the program but asked me to give you the chance if you wanted to participate. Call me at this number if you have any questions. Bye."

It was just like my father to have his own funeral planned out. He was planful.

I was stuck here until Saturday. The good news was that there wouldn't be many distractions, and I could actually get some work done without all the meetings my supervisor, Natasha, loved to pile on us. I had a lot of reading to do.

The last voice mail was from Jerica Bradley. Jerica had a crusty smoker's voice that sounded chronically angry—which was basically true. She was one of those authors that every publisher wanted but no one wanted to work with. She was best kept in the basement writing books—not just so she could write more, but because her book signings usually left her readers offended and disillusioned. After meeting her, longtime fans would, out of principle, stop buying her books. Her torturous personality wasn't just reserved for her readers and publishers. She once walked out of *Today*'s greenroom just twelve minutes before her appearance for the stated reason that she didn't like their coffee selection, leaving me and her publicist, Hannah, to do damage control with the show's producers. Not surprisingly, she hadn't been invited back.

"Aaaah, Noel, it's Jerica. Your girl told me you were out. I dropped off my manuscript. I think it's good. What am I saying, I'm always good. Let me know when you've read it."

Jerica was the last of my authors—maybe the last author in the world—who still delivered paper manuscripts. I had asked her many times, pleaded with her, to just email them to me, but she wouldn't. I dialed her number. As usual, she answered on the first ring.

"Noel, honey, it's me. Jerica."

I know, I thought. *I called you.* "Good morning."

"It's afternoon, honey. Did you get my manuscript?"

"Not yet. I'm out of town. I haven't been in the office since Monday night."

"No, honey, that doesn't work for me, I dropped it off yesterday morning with your girl. Where are you?"

"I'm in Utah."

"Good Lord, what are you doing there?"

"My father passed away."

"Oh. That's a shame, isn't it? So, when will you be back? I want to know what you think of the rewrite. I tossed William to the scrap pile. I never liked the man. I think the flow's better. When do you get back?"

"I'm not sure yet," I said. "My father's funeral is Saturday."

"You won't be back until Saturday? Do I really have to wait that long? Trust me, there's nothing in Utah worth staying for."

"No, I won't be back until Sunday at the soonest. You know, you could always just email your manuscript to me and I'll read it today."

She groaned. "Oh, not that again. You know I don't do that."

"I've forgotten why that is."

"It's not how I do things. Just hurry back."

"I'll be back as soon as I can," I said.

"Good girl."

Jerica always hung up without saying goodbye. And I always felt like a dog when she said "Good girl." In fact, she'd say it to her dog and me in the same sentence. Her dog, Pinot, was a teacup Maltese poodle, which I was more familiar with than I'd like to be. Jerica lived in SoHo, so, on the rare occasions when she agreed to do a book tour, she did a fair number of signings in Manhattan. For local events it was customary for me to escort her, a responsibility I had fulfilled on more than a dozen unpleasant occasions. As I said earlier, she wasn't the kind of author a publishing house liked to parade.

Jerica insisted on bringing Pinot with her wherever she went, transporting the small ball of fur in her purse. The canine was clearly of much greater importance to her than her readers were, and it wasn't unusual for her to stop signing books to feed her. Once, at a particularly large and well-publicized signing that she was late to, I suggested that she wait to feed her dog until after the signing. She informed me—with indignation—that Pinot's breed (which, she frequently reminded me, was of royal descent and even written about by no less than Aristotle) suffered from hypoglycemia and needed to eat regularly to keep their blood sugar levels up.

It gets worse. She would brush the dog's teeth during the signing since, as I was also informed, Maltese are known for having dental problems. Twice I had to drive her to a dog dentist in New York. I'm not making this up.

If that wasn't enough, Jerica would occasionally let Pinot relieve herself on the bookstore carpet. (At least Amy Tan made her dogs wear diapers.) Once, a manager told her that dogs weren't allowed in the store and she responded by walking out, leaving almost three hundred fans standing in line. *It's how she does things.*

I called my editorial assistant, Lori. She had been with me for almost six months. "What's going on?" I asked.

"Not much." Her voice sounded tense.

"Are you okay?"

She paused a beat before answering. "Yeah. I'm fine. Just stressed."

"I get it," I said. "Speaking of stress, I just heard from Jerica."

"Yes, she brought her manuscript by. I left it on your desk."

"That's why she called. How was she?"

"Her usual," she said. "How's your father doing?"

"He passed away."

"Oh, I'm so sorry. When it rains it pours, doesn't it?"

Her response confused me. "Did something else happen?"

She hesitated. "No, just that."

"Good, because I don't need any more bad news," I said. "Oh, before I forget, would you email Baldacci and remind him that production is waiting to get his sign-off on his new box-set design, and publicity's waiting for his approval on the flap copy."

"I already did."

"Aren't you Ms. Efficient today."

"I do what I can. When are you coming back?"

"I'm thinking next Monday or Tuesday. Trust me, I'm not staying here a second longer than I have to."

"No rush. I've got things under control. We're doing fine without you."

That's not something anyone wants to hear. "Thanks."

"So, gotta run. I've got a meeting with Natasha. I'll see you when I see you."

Lori hung up first, something she never did. Maybe she was finally bucking for a promotion.

I took a shower, then, seeing as how I would be staying in the house for a few more days, foraged through the kitchen cabinets to see what food my father had on hand. There wasn't much. I made a short shopping list.

Fortunately, Wendy had told me where the car keys were, a detail I was grateful for and, frankly, considering the circumstances, a little surprised she remembered.

I went out and manually opened the small one-car garage and got in my father's car. My father kept his car immaculately clean; as usual, a pine-scented air freshener hung from the rearview mirror. My father was fairly tall, six feet and a couple inches, and I couldn't reach the pedals without moving the seat up.

The grocery store wasn't far. It was almost the same one I went to as a child. I say almost because it was the same location and building but had a new name and different gestalt. The store was now hip, with a large selection of organic foods, exotic fruits, and cheeses. There was also a full half-aisle devoted to Halloween, which was just a few days away—the same day as my father's funeral.

Halloween was an event in these parts. We'd had an unusually large number of trick-or-treaters on our street. We lived in one of those staid, middle-class neighborhoods where the houses were close together, providing maximum efficiency for trick-or-treating. It seemed like every year more children would come, many from other parts of the valley. Family vans parked all along Parleys Boulevard and almost filled the church parking lot. The combined hordes looked like a Halloween parade.

Our family had a Halloween tradition. My mother would make chili and soft breadsticks for dinner, then my father would take me out trick-or-treating, holding my hand as we walked the length of our street and a few streets east of ours—enough to fill my plastic jack-o'-lantern with candy.

Along with a bag of Halloween candy, I purchased the basics, some rice and vegetables, oatmeal, milk, artisan bread, Greek yogurt, cheddar slices, protein drinks, and some canned chili.

That evening I was chopping carrots for dinner when my phone rang. I answered without checking the number.

"This is Noel."

"Noel, this is Wendy. I was just calling to check up on you."

"Thank you. I'm doing okay."

"Good. Did you get my voice mail?"

"Yes. Sorry I didn't get back to you. I got distracted by work."

"That's okay. I'm about to send the program to the funeral home. Did you want me to add you to the service?"

"No. I'll just listen," I said. "Will you be participating?"

"I'll be reading the obituary. Maybe offering a personal eulogy."

"I'm sure it will be nice."

"I hope so. He deserves a nice send-off. I'll see you Saturday morning."

"Thank you. See you then."

Did my father really think I'd want to speak? I don't know what I'd say. In some ways it would be like eulogizing a stranger.

I went back to making dinner—a fried-rice recipe I'd picked up in Chinatown.

As I sat down to eat, I thought, *I could use a glass of wine,* knowing it wouldn't happen. My father never had alcohol in the house. Instead I had a Coke, which I assumed Wendy had left in the fridge since my father didn't drink soda either.

After dinner, I checked my emails. Still nothing from work. This was highly unusual. There were usually at least two or three group emails every day about some new company policy or a book being dropped.

I went to my father's bookshelf in the front room and picked one of his favorite go-to books—one I hadn't read yet. *Slaughterhouse-Five* by Kurt Vonnegut. There was a dollar bill in it. My father used dollar bills as bookmarks. I'm not sure where I fell asleep reading. I just remember something about "legs like an Edwardian grand piano," and "so it goes."

CHAPTER

three

Great editors do not discover nor produce great authors; great authors create and produce great publishers.

—*John Farrar*

THURSDAY, OCTOBER 29

I woke with a feeling of impending doom. Maybe that's what happens when you fall asleep reading *Slaughterhouse-Five*. Or maybe it was just my life.

I don't know why an early morning anxiety attack should have surprised me. I was in a strange bed, I had just gone through a divorce and a death, and I was getting kicked out of my apartment. I was basically checking my way down the official list of anxiety-provoking situations. All I needed now was to lose my job.

I was desperate to get back to New York, if for no other reason than to return to a little routine. And I needed to find an apartment. Put that on the list.

It was already past noon Eastern time when I checked my email. Again, there was nothing from work. There were two possibilities: either my employer was having a party without me, or the publishing house was respecting my privacy in a difficult time and I should regard their silence as a sign of respect. Why was I feeling so insecure?

I made myself a breakfast of oatmeal with craisins.* I thought of going out for a walk, but the kitchen windows were iced over, and I just didn't have it in me that morning to endure anything that cold. I went back to the couch to finish the Vonnegut book. There were many places where my father had folded the corners or highlighted lines in marker. A few places he wrote *HA, HA.* My father had a slightly warped sense of humor, but I laughed at each of his notations.

I had been reading for about an hour when my phone rang. It was a 212 prefix, a New York area code, which pleased me. *They haven't forgotten about me after all,* I thought. The number belonged to Natasha, my supervisor at the publishing house. I set down the book and lifted my phone. "Natasha, I'm so glad to hear from you."

She hesitated. "Noel? Are you okay?"

"I'm fine."

"Oh," she said, sounding a little confused. "I was told your father died."

I understood her confusion. I lowered my voice. "He passed away Tuesday. Who told you?"

"Lori told me. I wanted to offer my condolences."

---

* The greatest man-made fruit since the tangelo.

"Thank you. That's kind of you to call."

There was another hesitation, and then she said, "Actually, that's not the only reason I called." Her voice tightened. "I'm afraid I have some bad news. There's no easy way to say it, so I'll just say it. We're terminating your position."

"Terminating my position? What's wrong with my position?"

"By the HR book, I'm supposed to use that terminology, but you're too smart for HR games. The truth is, we're terminating *you*."

"I don't understand."

"You're being let go."

"No, that part I understand. I don't understand *why*, out of nowhere, you're firing me."

"Actually, it's not so out of nowhere. It's been coming for some time now. HR has a collection of complaints. They have for a while."

"Complaints? From whom? Christine? You know I don't get along with her. Or with any of her sycophants."

"It's not just your colleagues, Noel. It's your authors as well."

For a moment I was speechless. "Who?"

"You know I can't tell you that."

"Then at least tell me what I did."

Her voice took on an edge. "You want me to go down the list?"

"I think I'm owed that."

"All right," she said. "I jotted down a few of the complaints. 'You're not present.' 'You ignore suggestions and input.' 'You don't pay attention.' 'Your personal life is negatively influencing your work—'"

"You think?" I blurted out. "I caught my husband cheating on me, my father was dying . . ."

"Shall I continue?" she said.

"If there's more."

"There's more. 'You're unpleasant to work with.' 'You're condescending.' 'You're overly negative, you're mean, and you snap when you're contradicted or someone doesn't agree with you on the slightest point.'"

"I can't help it if I work with idiots."

Natasha didn't say anything. I guess my response proved her point. Finally, I said, "How long has everyone hated me?"

"No one hates you," she said. "At least, I don't. Look, I didn't call to attack you."

". . . But you did."

"I gave you what you asked for."

"My books have done well."

"For the most part."

"What does that mean?"

"A few of your authors might disagree. One told me that she finally just surrendered her manuscript before she was done so she didn't have to deal with you anymore."

"Who said that?"

"Again, I'm not going to throw anyone under the bus."

"Just me," I said. "I gave you my best work."

"No one is disputing your commitment or your talent. Just your manner. This is a people business, Noel. It's like there are actors in Hollywood who can't get parts because no one wants to work with them. Same here."

"Give me just one example."

She groaned. "All right. Two weeks ago you slammed the phone down on Camille LeCrux."

"She was being incredibly rude."

"She's a house author, Noel. Yes, she's petty, rude, and agonizingly demanding. She also happens to sell more than twenty-five million dollars in books a year. There's not a house in the world that would keep you after that. And yes, she went straight to Jonathan. He had to talk her off the ledge. I've never seen him so angry."

I was quiet. Jonathan was the president of the publishing house. Not someone whose radar you want to land on. At least, not in a negative way.

After a moment Natasha said in a softer, more sympathetic tone, "I read through all the complaints. There was one common denominator. They all say you're just too angry to work with."

I let the accusation sink in. "So you waited for me to leave so you could tell me by phone?"

"No, I was going to tell you Wednesday afternoon, only that morning you came to ask for time off because your father was dying. Not exactly the moment to drop a bomb on you. I was respecting your situation."

"I think respecting my situation would have been to be truthful to me."

"That's your way of seeing it." She paused, then said, "You really are angry, Noel. And I just delivered a big reason for you to be even angrier. I'm sorry."

My chest felt heavy. "Why did you call today? Why not wait until I returned?"

"When I heard that your father died, I called to tell you so you didn't have to run back, in case you needed to make long-term plans. I didn't want you to hurry back just so I could fire you."

For nearly a minute my thoughts were treading water. "Who's taking my authors?"

"You don't need to worry about that."

"What about Lori?"

"You don't need to worry about her either."

"Is she taking my job?"

"Again, not your concern."

I took a deep breath, trying not to cry. "Then I guess we're done."

"Almost. HR will be reaching out to you in the next few days with specifics of your termination. I made them delay that call until I could speak with you."

I closed my eyes tight. Finally, I said, "I still need to clear out my desk."

"I asked Lori to put your things in boxes. We'll keep them in storage for now. We can ship them if you like."

I sighed deeply. "All right."

"Look, this isn't any fun for me either. I've had your back for a long time. As a friend, or at least a former one, may I give you some advice?"

"If you must . . ."

"Do yourself a favor and don't make any big decisions right now. Give yourself some breathing room. With your divorce, your father, and now this, your life is in a major upheaval. Let the dust settle a little before you start off on your next course."

I considered her words. "Would you ever let me back?"

"Would you want to come back?"

"I don't know. I thought I did well there."

Natasha exhaled slowly. "Never say never, right? You're a good editor. Would I hire back the woman I first hired? In a heartbeat."

I swallowed back the emotion. "Thank you."

She was quiet a moment, then said, "All right. I'll let you go. Get some rest. You sound exhausted. And I meant what I said, Noel. Take some time to care for yourself."

CHAPTER

four

You must stay drunk on writing so reality cannot destroy you.

—Ray Bradbury

I felt as if the very forces of nature had conspired to destroy me. All I could think to do was run, literally as well as figuratively. I put on my sweats, coat and gloves, and went outside.

It was cloudy when I emerged from the house. The flowers someone had left were still on the porch, frozen and dead. There was no longer any reason to salvage them, so I carried them around to the side of the house and dropped them, vase and all, into the garbage can. I stretched lightly and then proceeded to run.

The street was quiet, the ambient sounds dampened by a layer of snow that fleeced the lawns and roofs but hadn't stuck to the roads or sidewalks. After my mother's death I began running almost every day. I ran the four hundred meters for the girls' track team before I was kicked off the team for honor code violations.

Habitually, I started out following the same route I had

back in high school. I ran half a block south to the church then west toward my old high school.

As I neared the school, memories flooded back. I don't know if the school was between classes but there were kids standing in the cold around the front doors, hardly any of them were wearing coats. They looked like they were fighting off frostbite. *Why don't teenagers wear coats anymore?* I was sounding sensible, like an old person. *Why ask why?*

I ran south, past the school, then crossed into the 110-acre Sugar House Park. I cautiously descended a steep, snow-covered hill, slipping just once, then at the base, ran straight until I caught up to the road that made a one-way circular tour of the park. I ran twice around the park, passing its barren pavilions and playgrounds.

On my way home, life hit me with a full-blown anxiety attack. My heart was pounding so fiercely that I gasped for breath. Was this what a heart attack felt like? I couldn't run, I couldn't even walk. I knelt down on a patch of grass and sobbed.

God, if there is such a thing, I thought, *why do you hate me?*

CHAPTER

five

Tears are words that need to be written.

—Paulo Coelho

When I finally stopped crying I looked up. An Asian couple, a man and woman, were standing across the road looking at me.

"Are you okay?" the man asked.

I sniffed. "Yes."

"Do you need help?" the woman asked.

"No. Thank you." I wiped my eyes with my arm. "I'll be okay."

"Okay," the man said. They walked away.

I walked the rest of the way back to the house. I don't know if I had ever felt so alone in my life. Natasha was right—I was angry. But I had every right to be. I never thought I had a great life, actually the contrary, but in spite of it all, I at least thought I had built something good. Now it was all tumbling down. I was turning thirty-one in December. I was getting older but going backward.

CHAPTER

six

Writers live twice.

—*Natalie Goldberg*

FRIDAY, OCTOBER 30

The next morning I didn't want to get out of bed. Being jettisoned back into the job market wasn't something I had remotely considered at this time in my life. I didn't even have a résumé.

The reason I was fired wasn't going to make job hunting easy. In spite of being a global enterprise, the New York publishing world is incredibly small. Before I was hired, there would be over-lunch discussions and off-the-record phone calls. There was a chance I would discreetly be black-balled.

Here I was, back to where I had started, beginning my life all over again. It's like that board game when someone lands on you and sends you back to Start.

I made myself a cup of coffee and then sat down to escape in a book. It was somewhere around noon when the doorbell rang.

I put on a robe and walked to the front door, opening it just enough to look out. A paunchy, middle-aged man with an excessively receding hairline was on the porch.

He wore a polyester suit with an unfashionably wide tie that looked like a Father's Day gift he felt obliged to wear. He carried a leather satchel tucked beneath his right arm. I noticed that his hand was tremoring.

I wondered what he was selling. Whatever it was, I didn't want it.

"May I help you?" I asked curtly.

He looked at me, his eyes blinking rapidly. "Excuse me, but you are Noel Book?" His voice was a little hoarse.

"Noel *Post*," I corrected. "What can I do for you?"

"I should have known that. Your father told me you'd kept your married name. I'm sorry to drop in on you like this, but I called the number I was given for you, but no one answered. My name is Christopher Smalls, I'm your father's attorney."

"My father passed away."

"Yes, I know. That's why I'm here." He cleared his throat. "I'm very sorry for your loss. Your father was a fine man."

"Thank you," I said, wondering how well he actually knew him.

"Your father said you lived out of town and didn't know how long you'd be in Salt Lake, so, per his instructions, I brought some legal documents that need to be signed. Your father didn't want to waste time; you know how he was."

"I'll take your word for it," I said.

The bluntness of my response changed his demeanor. "I

know this must be a difficult time for you, so if you'd like me to come back later, I understand."

"I'm okay," I said. "Hold on a moment. Let me get some clothes on." I shut the door on him, went to my room, pulled on my jeans and a long-sleeved blouse and sweater, then came back and opened the door. "All right, you can come in."

"Thank you." He stepped into the front room and I closed the door behind him.

"Would you like some coffee?"

"Uh, no thanks. I'm good. I'm trying to cut back on caffeine."

"I'm going to get some for myself." I motioned to the front room couch. "Have a seat."

"It would probably be better if we sat at the table. I have a few documents that need to be signed."

"Wherever you like." I went into the kitchen and poured my coffee, then brought it to the table. The lawyer was already seated. He had opened his satchel and laid out his papers in a few orderly piles. He looked up at me as I sat.

"Your name is Christopher?"

"Yes, ma'am. Christopher Smalls."

"How long have you been my father's lawyer?"

"I've worked with your father for more than ten years, when he hired me to draft his first will, which we updated just a few weeks ago." He lifted his pen. "So, in his will, your father left you everything he owned." He handed me a few papers. "We'll begin here. Your father didn't have a lot of liquidity, but he maintained a life insurance policy worth a million dollars, for which he named you the sole beneficiary."

"A million dollars? Why would he have that much coverage after my mother's death?"

The lawyer glanced down at his papers. "He actually increased the benefit after your mother's death." He looked up at me. "He did it for you."

The revelation surprised me.

"He also had a Roth IRA account with a little more than $115,000. I've got that account information right here, and these are the notarized transfer papers. He also owns the house outright, which he has left to you. We don't have a recent appraisal, but this is a prime location for mid-priced homes. There's a home on the street just behind you that went for four-thirty-five last month. We'll need to visit the title company to transfer it correctly."

"This is . . ." I looked up at him. "I didn't expect he would leave me anything."

"Small compensation for losing your father, of course. I'm sure you're already aware that he left you the bookstore."

I leaned back slightly. "Then he *did* leave it to me . . ."

"I'm sorry, I assumed you knew. Yes, he left the entire business to you, including its assets."

"Not to be crass, but is it worth anything?"

"He lived off it for thirty years. I know that he worked his tail off to keep it going, but it's profitable. And, from what he told me, as a whole, things are looking up for independent booksellers."

I had never once asked my father about the bookstore. Working with authors for a major publishing house, I knew too well the endangered-species status of most independent bookstores—suffering the same terminal fate as the record and video store.

"Along with the house, he left everything in it to you, including all his personal belongings, which includes his automobile, his Lladró and rare book collection."

I was aware of the sculptures but not the books. "What books?"

"I don't know exactly what they are, just that he has some valuable editions. He keeps them in a fire safe at the bookstore. There's also a safe in the house where he's stored some valuables. He put the combination to both safes in this envelope." He handed it to me.

"Is there anything in it? The safe, I mean."

"I don't know what specifically, but he was adamant that I get this to you. He said that some of his most valuable possessions were in his home safe."

"Do you know where the safe is?"

"I assume he wrote down the location with the combination. But even if he didn't, it's a small house. I'm sure you won't have too much trouble finding it." He rubbed his chin. "I know I just laid a lot on you, but have you considered your plans?"

"Things are a little fluid right now." *Fluid* was an apt adjective, as I was pretty much drowning. "If you had asked me two days ago, I would have told you I was going to sell everything and get out of Dodge."

Mr. Smalls looked up at me over his glasses. "You don't like your father's car? From my experience, a Dodge is a quality automobile."

"I meant Dodge the old western town." Nada. "I meant I was going to leave Salt Lake."

"Of course." He frowned. "As your attorney, I would suggest you give yourself a little time to think that over."

Echoes of Natasha. "Are you my attorney?"

He hesitated. "That's up to you, of course. But your father hired me to represent your interests. So, if your plans are still to 'get out of Dodge,' I'd counsel you to postpone your asset liquidation and departure for at least a few months. Winter is never the best time to sell a house, and looking over the bookstore's financials, I noticed that more than thirty percent of the store's annual sales take place between Thanksgiving and Christmas. So, if I were giving you business advice, I'd suggest you at least ride it out until Christmas before selling it or shutting it down.

"Something else to consider, if you do decide to shut down, that would mean letting your father's most loyal employees go just a few weeks before Christmas. Maybe that doesn't matter to you, but it would to your father."

"I wouldn't do that," I said. Considering that I'd just been fired, the idea of doing that to someone else didn't appeal to me.

"So these are the documents you need to sign," he said, pushing a small stack of papers toward me.

"Do you have a pen?" I asked.

"Right here." He took one from his coat pocket. His hand tremored as he handed it to me. The pen was plastic and had his name on it. I went through the papers, signing each of them. After I finished, I handed him back his pen.

"You can keep the pen," he said magnanimously.

"Thank you."

He gathered one of the document piles into his satchel. "I'll get these filed with the state on Monday." He took the second pile and put it in a manila envelope and handed it to me. "These are for your records. I recommend you keep them someplace safe. Perhaps your new safe."

"Thank you," I said. "How do I get the insurance money?"

"I'll take care of that. It usually takes thirty to sixty days. But I've already sent in the documentation, so I'd expect it around the first of December at the earliest. If you'd like a direct deposit, I'll need your bank account and routing information. You can either email or text it to me."

"A check will be fine."

For the first time he smiled. "That will be an awfully big check," he said. "I'd like to see the look on the bank teller's face when you hand it to him." He stood uneasily, then walked to the door, stopping before opening it. "You should know that your father was more than a client to me. He was a friend. A few years ago, I went through some really hard times. I was diagnosed with Parkinson's. On top of that, my wife left me. Your father was there for me. He gave me a book I'll never forget—*Man's Search for Meaning*." He looked back at me. "Taking care of you is one way I can pay him back for all his kindnesses." He handed me a business card. "I'm sure you'll have some questions later. If there's anything I can do for you, just call."

"Thank you."

"It's my pleasure." He walked out the door, grasped the handrail, and carefully stepped down from the porch onto the slushy walk. I shut the door behind him. Then I leaned back against it and breathed out heavily. Just days ago I had left New York with every intention of returning as soon as possible. Now there was literally no reason to go back.

For years, my father had tried to get me to move back to Utah. Now he'd created roots to keep me here. Roots or chains? Maybe there wasn't a big difference between the two.

Whether that was my father's intention or not, the lawyer and Natasha were right. It made no sense to rush things. For now, I would surrender to the universe and see where it took me.

CHAPTER

seven

Outside of a dog, a book is a man's best friend.
Inside of a dog, it's too dark to read.
—Groucho Marx

I wondered what was in the safe. The lawyer had said that my father considered its contents among his most valuable possessions. I got the envelope from the table with the safe's combination. There were instructions to both safes along with their combinations.

> *House safe. Left side of bedroom closet. Bookstore,*
> *fire safe, office, South corner, Wendy.*

I guess that meant Wendy knew where the office safe was. I went to his bedroom and opened the closet. His clothes—myriad shirts, slacks, and three suits—still hung inside. On the left side of the closet were banker boxes and a guitar case with my father's Martin guitar. I pulled them away from the wall to reveal the safe, then set the paper with the instructions on the floor.

Home Safe
23 R – 32 L – 51 R

My first attempt at opening it wasn't successful, which didn't surprise me. In my experience, safes were hard to get into even with the combination. My ex-husband had a safe and not once had I gotten into it, though I've since considered that he had purposely given me the wrong combination. He had secrets.

I spun the dial around a few times to clear it, then tried again without success. I tried a third and fourth time, each time more carefully moving the dial, before finally giving up and deciding to try again later.

CHAPTER

eight

A writer's job is to give us moments that last a lifetime.

—Robert McKee

SATURDAY, OCTOBER 31

A funeral isn't a whole lot different from a book signing—except there are no books, no signing, and not a lot of author interaction. It didn't surprise me that my father had planned his own funeral. It would have been a surprise if he hadn't. My father was an event planner extraordinaire. It came naturally to him. One of the quotes he dropped on me from time to time was "Those who fail to plan are planning to fail."

I remember a book signing my father had held with a new author named James Redfield. Redfield had just released a book called *The Celestine Prophecy*. My father had an instinct about books, and he had scheduled the signing months before the book became a blockbuster bestseller. By the time the book signing came around, *The Celestine Prophecy* was the best-selling book in the country, maybe even the world.

More than three thousand people turned out for a book signing at our little bookstore that barely held fifty people. Even the local press showed up. I remember watching the cameramen walk up and down the line interviewing excited attendees.

My father was prepared with extra staff, streamlined book purchasing beneath tents outside the store, and stanchioned-off lines to control the crowds. The event came off flawlessly, and my mother reported that even Redfield claimed to be impressed.

My father had planned his funeral as meticulously as that book signing, though I'm pretty sure he was unhappy about having to pass it off to someone else for execution. That someone was Wendy.

I left the house a few minutes before nine, walking less than a block to the church where his funeral was being held. There was a sleek black hearse backed up to a side door, with the mortuary's name emblazoned on the side.

To my surprise, there was a line of cars on the street waiting to turn into the church parking lot. My first thought was that the church was simultaneously hosting two events. My father, as I remembered him, had always been a quiet man and a bit of a homebody, less happy in a crowd than reclined in his easy chair with a book. I had no idea my father even knew this many people.

I stomped the snow off my feet then walked into the church. There was already a line of mourners that stretched the length of the main church corridor before disappearing around a corner. I walked up to the door where the line fed into the room with my father's casket. Standing by the door was an older, silver-haired man wearing a black suit with a gold badge that read BEARD MORTUARY. The man put out his arm to stop me from entering.

"Excuse me, ma'am, the line for the viewing starts around that corner," he said. "Some of these people have been waiting for several hours."

I looked at him incredulously. "I'm his daughter."

"You're whose daughter?"

"Robert Book's," I said. "The deceased."

The man flushed. "I'm so sorry. Please, go right in."

I shook my head. Just another reminder that I was an outsider. I pressed my way into the crowded room.

Most of the mourners were my father's age, but not all. The people gathered were as eclectic as the books he sold. With the exception of somber whispers of consolation, the room was quiet. It was a far cry from the last funeral I'd been to. Three years earlier I had gone to a wake for my ex's uncle. The service was held at a country club with an open bar. The noise level grew so loud with laughter and chatting that it was hard to talk without shouting. At one point a fight broke out. It seemed to me that the casket and its occupant were little more than a conversation piece at a frat party. I said something about it to Marc, but he just said, "You know Stan. He would have wanted it that way."

The line to my father's casket followed the perimeter of the room. Against the walls were tables set up with an array of photographs, books, and other knickknacks from my father's life.

There were pictures of my father as a young man. It struck me how handsome he was, something a child rarely thinks about a parent. There were pictures from Vietnam, none of which I had ever seen. In one he was shirtless and holding a machine gun with ribbons of bullets crossing his chest. It was as ironic a portrayal of him as I could imagine.

There were myraid pictures of him and my mother—at least six from their wedding day. They looked like children. They practically were, as they married in their early twenties, almost ten years younger than I was.

There were pictures of our family, the three of us. Those were halcyon days. In one picture I was maybe four or five, walking between my parents, each of them holding a hand. There was a picture of me and my dad at my mom's funeral. I don't know who took the picture. I don't know why they took the picture.

In addition to the photographs there were books. Many of my father's favorites were on display, as if he were still trying to recommend them after his death. I walked over to the table to look through them. Most significant to me was Cervantes's *Don Quixote*. It was the perfect book to represent my father. He was always tilting at windmills.

I assumed the displays had been put together by Wendy. I looked around for her. She wasn't hard to find. She was standing next to the casket, her eyes red, talking to someone I didn't know. Actually, besides her, I didn't know anyone.

My father's casket lay against the east wall. It was partially open, the lid raised from his chest up—half-couch, they call it. The lower half of the casket was draped with a beautiful crimson spray of flowers. Red roses, red gerbera daisies, and red carnations, stark against the casket's varnished rosewood veneer.

The casket was nice, which made me think that it was probably chosen by Wendy, as my father would never have

RICHARD PAUL EVANS

chosen, or allowed, such reckless vanity. I once heard him go off on a diatribe about people building monuments to themselves after attending the funeral of a local author.

He used to say to my mother, *Just put me in a cardboard box and bury me in the backyard.* I used to hate it when he said that, but I'm not sure he was joking. He did, however, stop saying it after my mother died. And, I remembered, she had a beautiful casket, if there is such a thing.

My mother's was a unique funeral, different from most. I remembered that after the ceremony we all walked outside and released butterflies.

I've never liked the idea of a viewing. The idea of people filing past my dead body is disturbing to me—like strangers rummaging through my personal items at a garage sale. Considering that scientists have done studies to see if you spill less coffee walking forward or backward and why older men have big ears (I'm not making this up), I'm sure someone has done research to see if the practice of displaying the dead is psychologically valuable or damaging.

I can see that there might be a benefit to the tradition, as I've read that it provides finality to those left behind. I understand this. Because of the nature of the car accident, my mother's casket was closed. A part of me desperately wanted to pry open the box and see if she really was inside.

Wendy turned her attention to me as I approached the casket. I looked down at my father's lifeless body. The person inside the silk-lined box didn't look like my father. My father was never still. He was less matter than energy.

Nestled on top of the spray was a picture of my father, my

mother, and me. I was wearing a tutu and ballet slippers. I remembered the moment. I had just come from the *Nutcracker* tryouts and we were going out for ice cream. As I looked at the picture, I felt a hand on my back.

"I'm sorry," Wendy said. Her eyes were wet. Even more than mine. She handed me a tissue.

"Did you put together the table displays?" I asked, wiping my eyes.

"Your father told me what he wanted."

"Of course he did," I said.

"I'll bring everything back next week."

A half hour later the man from the mortuary said, "Ladies and gentlemen, the time has come. We'll soon be closing the casket and moving into the chapel for the service. If anyone would like to pay their last respects, now would be the time."

I walked back up to the casket. I had returned to Utah to see my father, and here he was. This wasn't the reunion I'd expected.

As I looked at him, I was suddenly flooded with memories, rising up in my psyche like groundwater. I remembered a hundred moments together, the times he held my tiny hand on walks, the magic of Christmas morning, his slipping the frosting from his birthday cake onto my plate when my mother wasn't looking. I remembered him tossing me in the air as I screamed with delight and demanded it again and again until his back hurt.

Tears streamed down my face. For the first time since I learned of his death, I felt the anguish of grief, just as I had with my mother. I didn't want to hurt like that again. I wanted to bolt from the place. I wanted to run all the way back to New York. I took a deep breath and said, "Rest in peace, Dad. I hope you find peace."

I grabbed another tissue from a box next to the casket. As I turned back, I saw that almost everyone in the room was looking at me. I was embarrassed to suddenly be the center of attention. I quickly moved away.

Someone else came forward—an older woman I had never seen before. It was obvious that she was deeply grieving. But even in her grief, she moved with elegance. She was exceedingly thin, pretty, with short, dark hair pulled back tightly, exposing the graceful curvature of her forehead. Her high-boned cheeks were streaked with mascara and her eyes, even with the pain they carried, were beautiful, large and deep set. She was immaculately dressed, like the well-heeled women from the West Village. She reminded me of Audrey Hepburn in her later years.

The woman reached into the casket and gently touched my father's arm. For a moment she just looked at him. Then she leaned forward, whispered something in his ear, and kissed his cheek. She slid a book into the casket, then stepped back. I turned to ask Wendy who the woman was, but she was already on the other side of the room. Actually, I was more curious to find out what the book was and why she thought he needed it.

The man from the mortuary looked around to see if anyone else was coming forward, and then he and his associate closed the top half of the casket. There was an audible gasp of emotion. And just like that, my father was gone.

CHAPTER

nine

If my doctor told me I had only six minutes to live . . .
I'd type a little faster.

—Isaac Asimov

The dark-suited men from the mortuary rolled the casket into the chapel, followed by a small procession led by Wendy and me. There was no other family. My father had one sister, but she had come down with MS and had passed away several years prior. I had missed that funeral.

To my amazement the chapel was filled to capacity and the dividers at the back of the room were open to accommodate the overflow. At each of the doors people were handing out programs or ushering mourners inside. One of them handed me a program as I entered the chapel.

"Who are all these people helping?" I asked Wendy.

"They're from the Sugar House Rotary Club," she said. "Your dad was a member."

Everyone stood as we entered the chapel and remained standing until we had walked to the front pew and sat down just a few yards from the casket and the lectern above it. After we were seated a man walked forward wearing the robe of a pastor.

"Good morning," he said. "My name is Dave Nelson. I'm the pastor of this church. We've gathered here today to celebrate the life of a great man. Or, I should say, a man's life lived greatly. The attendance here today speaks volumes to the kind of life Robert Book lived.

"In Ecclesiastes, the preacher taught, 'There is a time for everything, and a season for every activity under the heavens: a time to be born and a time to die, a time to plant and a time to uproot . . . a time to weep and a time to laugh, a time to mourn and a time to dance.'

"Today is a time for us to weep and mourn. But not for long. Our Savior counseled, 'Do not let your hearts be troubled. You believe in God; believe also in me. My Father's house has many rooms; . . . I go there to prepare a place for you, I will come back and take you to be with me that you also may be where I am.'"

The pastor looked out over the congregation. "We can only hope there are many books in Robert's room." There was a soft chorus of pious laughter.

"We are comforted to know that Robert Book is not alone. He was preceded in death by his beloved wife, Celeste. He will be followed in death by all of us. As we still have time, let us use it wisely and live such that our deaths may too be sweet. May God bless you with his eternal peace."

The pastor was followed by a soloist, a thirtysomething woman with a beautiful, operatic voice. She sang the hymn "How Great Thou Art."

The reading of the obituary was done by Wendy. She was, as I expected, emotional, and had difficulty getting through the short reading, even though she'd written the obituary herself. I think she'd planned on saying more but was too emotional to continue, so she returned to her seat instead.

After Wendy sat down, the woman from the viewing—the well-dressed one who had approached the casket after me—walked up to the lectern. I looked down at the program to see who she was. Her name, appropriately, was Grace.

It was immediately clear to me that she knew my father well, as she spoke of things I didn't know about him. She ended her eulogy by reading a quote from one of my father's favorite authors.

"The author John Steinbeck wrote," she said, looking down at a piece of paper, "'It seems to me that if you or I must choose between two courses of thought or action, we should remember our dying and try so to live that our death brings no pleasure to the world.'" She looked up. "There is no pleasure in our farewell. Robert's death is a loss to all who knew him." She furtively glanced down at me then back out at the crowd. "He was, simply, one of the finest men I've ever known. It was an honor to be counted among his many friends." She teared up. "Godspeed, my dear one." She slowly turned and walked back to the chair she'd risen from.

A moment later an older Black man dressed in an Army Service Uniform walked up to the lectern. He spoke briefly about their service together in Vietnam and the occasion on which my father had been awarded a bronze star with a "V" device for valor under fire. I had no idea my father had been given the medal. That's how tight-lipped he was about his service.

Afterward, the pastor stood and gave the benediction.

"The God of peace, who brought again from the dead our Lord Jesus Christ, the great Shepherd of the sheep, through the blood of the everlasting covenant: Make you perfect in every good work to do his will, working in you that which is well-pleasing in his sight; through Jesus Christ, to whom be glory forever and ever. Amen."

This concluded the service. The funeral director gave instructions to the congregation and the casket was lifted by a half dozen pallbearers who carried it outside to the waiting hearse. I followed the casket out. After the casket was in the car, one of the pallbearers—the man who had served in the war with my father—approached me. "Noel, my name is Steve Johnson," he said, handing me a business card. "If there's anything you need, anything at all, you just call. Your father was there for me. It would be a sincere honor to return the favor."

"Thank you."

"No, thank your father." He turned and walked away. I looked at the card. Mr. Johnson was the owner of a trucking company.

There is a rarely used word that described the moment to me: *apotheosis*. It means the deification of mortals. I think it's natural, especially at funerals, for people to make the deceased more than they were in life—only my father's funeral felt a little different. The people around me seemed sincere in their praise and love for my father. And, like Wendy, they were authentic in their grief.

After the service, the cars lined up to drive to the cemetery for the burial.

"Are you going to join the procession?" Wendy asked.

"I need to go home and get the car," I said. "I'll meet you up there."

"Do you know where the cemetery is?"

"It's the same plot where my mother's buried."

"Of course. I'll see you there."

I walked home, got into my father's car, and drove to the cemetery. My mind was still reeling with what I'd just experienced. My father had either done a remarkable job of fooling the masses or he had changed a lot since my childhood.

When I arrived at the cemetery I parked in the nearest space I could find, which was at least three hundred yards from the grave, and walked up the slick, snow-banked street to the gathering. The snow had been cleared from the site and artificial turf had been laid around the opening in the ground. The granite headstone was already in place. It had been there, with my father's name on it, for almost twenty years, ever since my mother died.

I watched as the pallbearers struggled up the snowy hillside, laid the casket down, and then removed their boutonnieres and placed them on the casket's lid.

In front of the casket was a canopied "portachapel" sheltering about twenty folding chairs. Wendy had saved a seat for me in the center of the front row. Also in the front row, two seats from Wendy, was the woman Grace. The graveside service was brief; the pastor said a simple prayer and then dismissed the crowd. As I got up to go Wendy said to me, "We'll need to discuss your plans for the bookstore before you leave town."

"Of course."

"When you're ready."

I walked back to my car alone and drove home.

When I got back to the house, there were three large boxes on the front porch. I checked their shipping labels. They had come from my publisher. I could guess what was inside. Natasha had sent my things from my office. Or, more likely, my assistant had, as it was Lori's signature on the labels. They hadn't wasted much time in removing the evidence of my former employment. According to the shipping date, my office had been cleared out the day after I'd left town. No wonder Lori had sounded so anxious when I called.

I brought the boxes inside, soaked a washcloth in warm water, and laid on the couch with the cloth over my face. There was far too much in my life right now to process. Most of all I just wanted to be left alone.

I had forgotten it was Halloween.

The onslaught started early, hours before dark. I gave up on trying to rest, made myself some chili, and grabbed a book. For the next three hours my reading was interrupted every few minutes by the doorbell, followed by shouts of "Trick or Treat."

Finally, I just put out what was left of the candy and turned out the porch light. It was a surreal ending to an already surreal day.

CHAPTER

ten

A blank piece of paper is God's way of telling us how hard it is to be God.

—Sidney Sheldon

SUNDAY, NOVEMBER 1

I woke the next morning with an emotional hangover. I drank a black coffee, then went out and ran to clear my mind. With the funeral over, it was time for me to figure out what I was going to do. In the last two months I'd lost my marriage, my apartment, my father, and now my job. Maybe this was how women ended up as cat ladies. It's a good thing I was allergic to cats.

Running had neither cleared my mind nor my lungs, as the overcast sky was more brown than gray from one of the valley's inversions. The weather only added to my feelings of suffocation beneath the weight of anxiety and loneliness.

I bathed and dressed, then drove up the canyon to Park City to get out of the inversion. It was still early in the ski season, but there was enough snow to attract skiers and the resorts' parking lots were full. Seeing the crowds only made me feel lonelier.

It occurred to me that if I died at the house, it might be days, or weeks, before anyone found me. My only "friends" were people I worked with. At least I'd thought they were friends. More than likely, Lori had provided testimony for my termination, and Natasha had dropped the axe. And my former colleague, Diana, had kicked me out of our apartment. I really didn't blame her for this—I was happy that she was working things out with her husband—it was just that the timing was unfortunate. There wasn't a single person in my life whom I'd called a friend who wasn't in some way distancing themselves from me.

This wasn't the first time I'd felt this way. After my mother's death, I'd felt like a loner for most of my life. Maybe that's why I spent so much time lost in books. As Hemingway said, "There is no friend as loyal as a book." But I knew better. I needed something more than paper. I needed to be around people. Looking back on this moment much later, I suppose that's the reason I hired myself at the bookstore.

CHAPTER

eleven

I love walking into a bookstore. It's like all my friends are sitting on shelves, waving their pages at me.

—Tahereh Mafi

MONDAY, NOVEMBER 2

My father's bookstore was located just a few miles north of the house, in what had become a trendy section of the city. It sat on the corner of Ninth and Ninth, across the street from a gelateria, a bread bakery, and a touring bicycle shop.

His store resembled an old English bookstore, with myriad-paned windows revealing carefully themed book displays. A sign hung across the front of the store:

BOBBOOKS

I pulled into the store's snow-plowed parking lot and parked in a vacant space beneath a sign that read

Reserved for Robert Book

There was an employee entrance in back, which I tried but found locked. I knocked a few times but no one answered, so I walked around to the front. A brass shopkeeper's bell rang as I opened the door.

Entering was a wonderful assault to the senses. The store smelled of lavender, sage, and old leather. Instrumental harpsichord Christmas music filled the air as richly as the fragrances.

It had been many years since I'd entered the old store. It had aged well, and those things that had once seemed outdated and old were now vintage and classic. My father had always had an artistic flair, but only now did I understand that the bookstore was the canvas on which he expressed it. On every vacation we took as a family my father would visit the local bookstores, always talking to the proprietors and coming back with a list of new ideas to implement in his own store.

Even with its struggles, the book business had a rich culture, and my father was one of its guardians as the digital waves of online consumerism crashed around him.

The store's shelves were all varnished oak and strategically placed like a labyrinth, creating small nooks and crannies. Comfortable, well-worn old chairs were scattered about for people to sit in as they perused their books.

One bookshelf ran along a brick wall covered with English ivy that had grown and established itself in the time I'd been gone. There were book displays made from old wine barrels.

Along one side of the store the shelves went all the way to

the ceiling, and there were ladders on brass railings that slid down the length of the wall to reach the upper books.

The place was magical.

Near the front door was a small display shelf with a sign that read ROBERT'S FAVORITES.

Hanging from chains above the shelf was a hand-painted sign on stained, weathered wood.

Live in the sunshine, swim the sea, drink the wild air.
—Emerson

My father's "favorites" were about as eclectic a gathering of literature as might be found anywhere: *East of Eden, Cannery Row, The Firm, The Color Purple, The Great Gatsby, Catch-22, The Brothers Karamazov, The Picture of Dorian Gray, Alice's Adventures in Wonderland, For Whom the Bell Tolls,* and *Brave New World.*

"Hello."

I turned to see Wendy, who had just emerged from the back. She was wearing a bright green sweater, bright crimson lipstick, and red leggings. She looked gorgeous, and still a little fragile. "It's my elf outfit," she said, anticipating my reaction. "Your father always embraced the holidays on the first of November. This is my homage."

"I'm sure he appreciates it."

"I'm sure he does too," she said. "So did you come to check out your bookstore?"

"When did you know he was leaving it to me?"

"He told me a few months ago." She put her hands on her hips. "How long has it been since you've been here?"

"It's been about sixteen years."

"That's a chunk of time. It's probably changed a little."

"It's changed a lot," I said. "Or maybe I forgot what it looked like."

"May I help you with anything?"

"Actually, I came to help you."

Her eyebrows rose. "Yes?"

"I figured as long as I'm here, I might as well work."

"You're not headed back to New York?"

"Not for a while. I'll probably be staying until the New Year."

Wendy looked at me as if she were processing what that meant. I couldn't tell if she was happy with the idea. "You want to work here through the holidays?"

"If that's okay with you."

"We could definitely use the help," she said. "Besides, it's your store . . ."

"About that," I said. "I may be the owner on paper. But you know how things run. I don't want to get in your way. This is more your store than mine. You built it."

"Your father built it."

"With your help," I said. "So, when I said I came to help, I meant it. You're the boss. Put me to work."

She looked at me skeptically. "You're saying I'm the boss?"

"That's the deal."

"All right. We'll see how that goes."

"What can I get started on?"

"I just got in a shipment of books, so if you wouldn't mind watching the front, I can start unpacking."

"You want me to just stand here?"

"Basically. If someone comes in, you can help them find something. As a side benefit, it keeps shoplifting down."

"Do we have a lot of theft?"

"Not a lot. But we live on thin margins, and they usually try to return what they stole to us."

"That's ironic."

"What's ironic is the most stolen book is the Bible. And anything by Kurt Vonnegut."

"I don't see the connection."

"There isn't one."

"My father loved Vonnegut."

Wendy smiled as if I were telling her something she knew better than I did. "I know."

"So what do we do if someone tries to return something we think they stole?"

She pointed to a small sign taped to the cash register. "No receipt, no returns."

"Won't they just take it somewhere else?"

"Yes. But at least we got them out of the store. And most thieves are lazy. They'd rather just take their loot back to where they got it. So, hopefully, they'll go somewhere else next time."

I looked over at a young woman perusing a row of books in the self-help section. "She looks like a thief," I said facetiously.

"Only technically," Wendy said. "She's *showrooming*."

"What's showrooming?"

"It means she's using our store as a showroom. She checks out the books she's interested in, then after she leaves, she'll buy them online, where she can get them for less. Sometimes they don't even wait to leave the store."

"How can you tell?"

"She keeps taking pictures of books."

I looked back over at the woman. She was holding her phone up to a book. She saw us looking at her and put her phone down. Wendy turned back to me. "So, in the unlikely event that her perusing turns to purchasing, do you know how to take payment?"

"No."

"It's not hard. I'll show you this afternoon. In the meantime, you can come get me."

"Is there anything else you need me to do?"

She looked around. "I need to change that table display of Halloween books to holiday books. Do you have any experience with displays?"

"I'm sure I could figure it out."

She looked unconvinced. "Tell you what—just take the books off the table and stack them on the floor for now, then take the books out of those boxes and put them on the table. I'll finish up later. If you have any questions, you know where to find me." She walked to the back of the store.

I began taking the books off the table. There were four boxes marked CHRISTMAS BOOKS. They were mostly classic Christmas tales.

We had more than a dozen customers over the next three hours, more than I expected. A little after noon I found Wendy in the back. "What do you do for lunch?"

She lifted a brown paper sack from her desk. "My lunch plans are right here. I thought I was working alone this morning, so I brown bagged it."

"I think I'll walk over to that bread place and get something."

"Is there anyone up front?"

"There are currently two customers."

"Okay. I'll come out."

"I'll see you in a half hour." I stopped at her door. "Maybe we could go to lunch sometime."

She looked a little surprised at the invitation. "That would be nice. Thank you."

The bread store was crowded. I ate my lunch with a stranger (we shared the last open table), then walked back to the bookstore.

In the short time I was gone, Wendy had arranged the Christmas book display I'd begun and was now hanging a string of lights in the front window. There was an artificial Christmas tree lying in sections on the floor next to the front desk, along with two bins filled with Christmas decorations.

"You've been busy," I said.

"'Tis the season."

"Did you eat lunch?"

"Almost."

There were three customers in the store. A man was looking through the history shelves, while a woman perused our *New York Times* bestsellers shelf. She was holding one of Jerica Bradley's books, one I had edited. I was considering telling her that I had worked on the book when she put it back.

I recognized the third customer. She was the elegant woman who had spoken at my father's funeral. *Grace*, I reminded myself. I wasn't absolutely positive it was her, as she was wearing glasses and a hat and was dressed much more casually than before, though she was still dressed up by my standards. Over her shoulder was a debossed cream-colored

Louis Vuitton tote.

I walked up to her. "May I help you?"

She looked at me and smiled. "Hi, Noel."

I was surprised that she knew my name. "You spoke at my father's funeral."

She extended her hand. I took it.

"My name is Grace Kingsbury. Your father was a dear friend of mine. I'm sorry we didn't speak on Saturday. I wanted to share my deepest condolences."

"Thank you," I said. "I should have introduced myself. I wasn't feeling very social. But I thought your eulogy was beautiful."

"That's kind of you. I deeply admired your father. He was a remarkable man."

"How did you know him?"

"Circumstance," she said. "You probably don't remember, but you and I have met before." She smiled slightly. "I still remember the circumstance. You were a teenager and upset because your father wouldn't let you go to a party where they were serving alcohol. It was right here at the store. You were a bit agitated. You probably didn't even see me standing next to him."

"I can't believe you remember that."

"I have a good memory," she said. "I've been a regular at the bookstore for eighteen years. You're living in New York now?"

"Yes."

"Which borough?"

"Brooklyn. For the time being."

"For the time being. Are you planning on moving?"

"Not by choice. My roommate is kicking me out," I said. "She's getting back together with her husband." I'm not sure why I felt the need to explain. "It's fairly recent, so I don't know where I'll end up. For now I've decided to stay in Utah."

"Probably not a bad plan," she said. "If your publisher can give you the time off."

"That's not a problem," I said. I didn't ask how she knew I worked for a publisher.

"I love Manhattan in December. Except for all the tourists." She spoke like a resident. "You've lived there?"

"I studied dance at Juilliard," she said. "When I was young, of course."

"How did you end up in Utah?"

"My husband. We came west with his job. Before that we were living in Hartford. I've been all over Europe, but moving here was my first time west of the Mississippi."

"That must have been a culture shock."

"It wasn't bad. People are people, no matter where they live. And I was pleasantly surprised to find the people here were a bit softer."

"Softer?"

"Not as hardened by life as they were in New York."

"I can see that," I said. "Did you keep dancing?"

"A little. But I finally had to let it go."

"Why is that?"

"The thing that dooms every professional athlete, dear. Age. And, in my case, a child."

"I used to dance," I said. "When I was little."

"I know. It made your father very happy. He had a special place in his heart for dancers." She looked at me as if she were gauging my response. "Will you be working at the bookstore now?"

"I plan to. As long as Wendy doesn't throw me out."

"Wendy is a tad possessive," she said. "And quite particular. Though, I suppose, I'm equally guilty. I've learned not to reshelve the books, and she's learned not to suggest what I should read. I'm sure you'll do fine."

"I'm still getting to know her."

"She's a good girl," she said. "She was your father's right-hand woman. She's done a yeoman's job of keeping things running after your father fell ill." Her expression turned more intense. "So, if I may ask, what are your plans for your bookstore?"

My bookstore. It still sounded peculiar to me. "I don't know yet. I've got a lot of things to figure out."

"I'm sure you do. Working here will be good for you. It will help you find some clarity." She lifted the book she was holding: *The Devil in the White City* by Erik Larson. "I'd like to purchase this book."

"Very good." I walked around the counter to the register. Then I smiled. "I'm sorry. I have no idea how to ring you up."

"That's okay. You can just write it down and Wendy will ring me up later. That's what I used to do when your father was busy with other customers. You have my card on file."

"Let me find something to write on."

"There's a notepad in the drawer to the left of the register," she said. "There should be a mechanical pencil in there too. Your father always used pencils." She smiled. "It was a philosophical statement with him. He said it was a reminder that everyone makes mistakes."

I opened the drawer. As she said, there was a pad of paper

with the store's name printed at the top. I brought it out.

"It seems like everyone knows more about the store than I do. Even the customers."

"You'll catch up," she said.

I wrote down the name of her book along with its ISBN. "Your name is Grace . . ."

"Kingsbury. Like the Christian author. But you can just write down 'Grace.' I've been coming here for two decades. I'd be surprised if Wendy doesn't have my credit card memorized by now."

"Thank you . . . for your patronage."

She grinned. "Now you sound like your father. I'll see you next week."

She walked out of the store, the little bell ringing her departure. After she left, I helped another customer find two books—*American Sniper* and *The Five Love Languages*. I had to get Wendy to check him out.

"That was an interesting combination of books," I said after the man left.

Wendy grinned. "Maybe he's married and it's plan A and plan B."

I laughed. Then I looked at her and asked, "Are you married?"

"Nope."

"Dating?"

"Nope." From the curtness of her response I could tell she didn't want to talk about it.

"As long as we're here," she said, "I might as well teach you how to use this thing. It's not hard."

I found the paper with Grace's name. "We can practice on this one," I said. "It's from Grace. She said you had her information."

"Yes we do. She's purchased a book here every week since

even before I started."

"That's a lot of books."

"Probably a thousand."

"Why doesn't she just go to the library?"

"So we can survive," she said. "She can afford it. You know that bag she carries?"

"The Louis Vuitton?"

She nodded. "It cost more than three thousand dollars. If you have that much money for a book bag, you have money for books." She stepped in front of the register. "So, let me show you how this works." As she was showing me she asked, "How long were you planning on staying?"

"At least until Christmas."

She smiled. "I meant today."

"Oh. I wasn't sure. How late are we open?"

"Until ten during the holidays. As your father used to say, *It's harvest time.*"

"How late do you stay?"

"I usually work eight thirty to five thirty. I come in a little early to get the store open and stay a little late to hand off the baton." She suddenly smiled. "Sometimes I'd work late just to hang out with your father. We got into the most interesting conversations."

"About what?"

"Have you ever talked to your father about UFOs?"

"No."

"That's a conversation you won't soon forget."

"I don't think we'll be having that conversation," I said. "Or any other."

Her smile fell. "No, you won't." She changed the subject.

"We have two part-time workers who come in at five. Cammy and Cyndee. They're university students. After Thanksgiving we'll bring on two more part-time employees to work evenings. It gets pretty busy."

"I'm surprised at how much business you do."

"*We* do," she said. "We do a brisk business."

She was about to leave when I said, "Can I ask you something?"

She looked back. "Yes?"

"What was the relationship between Grace and my father?"

Wendy didn't answer immediately. I sensed there was a history between the two women. "They were friends," she finally said. "Why do you ask?"

"They seemed close."

"They were close. Your father asked her to speak at his funeral."

"Did she visit him while he was dying?"

"Every day."

"Were they in love?"

From her expression I sensed that she didn't like the question. After a moment she said, "They were close."

I decided it was best to leave it alone. "Were you with my father a lot? While he was sick?"

"Can this be the last question about him for now?" she asked.

"Yes. I'm sorry."

"The last five weeks I ran the store and then went to his house after work. The last two, I was with him all day, every day."

"He was lucky to have you."

"He wasn't the lucky one." She slowly exhaled. "I'm going

to finish decorating. We always got the Christmas decorations up the first day of November."

"Do you need some help?"

"No. Just watch the front."

I stayed behind the register while Wendy went back to decorating. She didn't look at me, and I noticed her wiping her eyes.

CHAPTER

twelve

There is nothing to writing.
All you do is sit down at a typewriter and bleed.

—Ernest Hemingway

Before going home that night I asked Wendy about my father's book collection. I brought out the paper with the combination. "The lawyer said my dad has some valuable books. I brought the combination to the safe."

"You won't need that; I had to memorize the combinations because I could never read his writing. His handwriting was bad enough, but his numbers . . ." She shook her head for dramatic effect. "His fives look like Ss, his sevens look like ones, and his ones look like twos. More than once we got the wrong number of books because the sales rep misread his writing. I finally convinced him to let me do the ordering."

We walked back to the office. Wendy locked the door behind us. "There are two safes."

"Why two?"

"This one," she said, motioning to a large black safe with a slot in front, "is for cash. It's where we keep the money at night."

"And the other?"

"It's where your father keeps his collection." She lifted a drape that hung over the second safe, concealing it. "He figured that if we were ever robbed, the thieves would see the one safe and assume that was it. Pretty clever."

"Have you ever been robbed?"

"Not yet." She squatted down next to the safe and dialed the combination. She opened the thick door, revealing a stack of books. "Would you like to see them?"

"Yes, please."

Wendy put on a pair of cotton gloves that were in the safe next to the books. They were much too large for her hands, so I guessed they belonged to my father.

The first book she brought out was *Cup of Gold* by John Steinbeck. She set it down on her desk. I didn't know the book but I did, of course, know the author. Steinbeck was one of my father's favorites. At a young age he had introduced me to *Cannery Row*, *Of Mice and Men*, and *East of Eden*.

"This was Steinbeck's first novel," Wendy said. "And this is a first edition. It's worth about twenty thousand."

She took out a second book, setting it down next to the Steinbeck.

I immediately recognized the cover. "*Atlas Shrugged*."

Wendy nodded. "Also a first edition. It's inscribed by Ayn Rand."

"What is that worth?"

"If I remember correctly, it's almost the same as the Steinbeck. Maybe a little less."

She reached back into the safe. "You'll like these." She

brought out two books. The spines were thick and embossed in gold leaf. "They're second-edition Elizabeth Barrett Browning poetry collections. They contain the first printing of the love poems she wrote to her husband, *Sonnets from the Portuguese.*"

I moved closer to examine them more carefully. As I reached out to touch them she stopped me. "You don't want to touch them with your fingers. Too much oil."

"Sorry."

"And last but not least." She reached back into the safe and pulled out another book. "*Death in the Afternoon.* A first-edition Hemingway, inscribed."

"What is that worth?"

"Much." She looked at me. "If you've ever wondered why your father didn't drive an expensive car, it's because he was smarter than most. He bought things that actually increased in value."

I was impressed by his collection. My collection.

"What do you want to do with them?" she asked.

"I'll keep them in the safe," I said.

"I thought you would." She returned the books along with the gloves and locked the safe.

"Now if I could just open the safe at home," I said. "Have you ever opened that one?"

She shook her head. "I've seen it, but I don't know what's inside."

I stayed long enough to meet the two evening-shift employees. Cammy was in her early twenties, an English major at the University of Utah. Cyndee was twenty-five, a business major with a Mandarin minor who was currently taking a break from school.

As I drove home, I thought about the books my father had collected. I wondered why he had never mentioned them to me. Considering how little we talked, I guess it wasn't high on his priority list.

I stopped to get groceries. The things I bought showed a little more commitment to staying; more oatmeal and granola, mayonnaise, Raisin Bran, a full gallon of skim milk, and a large bag of healthy popcorn. I put the groceries away then sat down on the couch to read. I was tired from standing on my feet all day, which was a good thing. At the publishing house I was getting used to spending the day on my rear.

As I reheated the fried rice from the day before, I thought about Wendy and the bookstore. I wondered if she planned to stay or was already scheming her exit. Or what she'd do if I ended up selling the place. Wendy was a bit of an enigma to me. She was smart, ambitious, and pretty, yet it seemed like she had no life outside of the bookstore. I didn't want to be the instrument that ended it all.

CHAPTER

thirteen

I can shake off everything as I write;
my sorrows disappear, my courage is reborn.

—Anne Frank

TUESDAY, NOVEMBER 3

I woke early the next morning. I went for my run then got ready for work. It felt good to have a routine again. I picked up a cappuccino on the way to work and arrived at the bookstore about a quarter after nine. Christmas music was playing, and there were new pleasant fragrances wafting through the store. Wassail and pine.

Wendy must have arrived extra early, as the store was noticeably more decorated than it was when I had left last night. The Christmas tree next to the front counter was up and decorated, strung with lights and baubles, each bearing a picture of a classic book: *Gone with the Wind*, *Ulysses*, *The Old Man and the Sea*.

As I hung my coat on the rack next to the cash register, Wendy walked in from the back. "You're late."

I couldn't tell if she was teasing or testing me on the whole "boss" thing, but either way, I fell in line. "Sorry. I'll be on time tomorrow. What's on the docket?"

"I just got another shipment of books," she said. "If you'll take the front, I'll check in the arrivals. We'll shelve them after lunch."

"You got it," I said. "The store looks nice."

"Thank you."

It was a quiet morning. Around noon a woman walked up to me at the counter. "Excuse me. Do you know who wrote *The Diary of Anne Frank?*"

She was looking at me so expectantly I decided she wasn't joking. "That would be . . . Anne Frank."

"Right. Of course. Do you know if she ever wrote a sequel?"

Now I was really wondering. I finally just said no.

"No, you don't know, or no, she never wrote one?"

"Have you read the book?"

"Yes. It was beautifully written. That's why I wanted to know if she'd written anything else."

I sighed "No. She wrote only the one book."

"That's a shame she didn't pursue her writing. She could have had a promising career. Thanks anyway."

I went in back and found Wendy. "You won't believe what someone just asked me."

"I've worked here for seventeen years. I'll believe anything. Try me."

"She asked if Anne Frank had written a sequel."

She grinned. "I've been asked that before." She looked up. "I think the most bizarre question was from a woman who asked if we had a book on avids."

"On what?"

"Avids," Wendy said. "The woman said, 'My husband is an avid hunter, and I thought he'd like a book on them for Father's Day.'"

"Tell me she was joking."

"For her sake I hoped she was, but she wasn't."

I shook my head. "Are people just dumb?"

"I think everyone's dumb. Just in different ways. Einstein used to get lost on the way home."

It was another busy day, and I could sense from our customers the growing anticipation of the holidays, like water rolling to a boil. The ambience Wendy created certainly helped. If you weren't in the Christmas spirit when you arrived at our shop, you would be by the time you left.

Businesswise, Wendy said we were doing well. I still hadn't gone through the store's financials—something I was as ill prepared to do without an accountant as hike through the Amazon without a guide—so I had no idea of the store's financial status. All I knew from the publishers' end of things were the ongoing reports of the demise of the independent American bookseller. Happily, in the case of Bobbooks, a line from Mark Twain seemed to apply: "Reports of my death have been greatly exaggerated."

I worked until seven thirty, taking just a short break for dinner, then came home a couple of hours after dark. I decided to read a little before going to bed, and I was a chapter into a new book called *Fates and Furies* when the doorbell rang.

It was a little late for visitors, especially since I didn't know anyone, and I had visions of Mr. Smalls, the attorney, standing on my doorstep. I got up and opened the door.

A man stood in the doorway. He was certainly no Smalls. He looked to be my age, tall, with light-brown wavy hair and the beginnings of a beard. He was wearing a leather bomber jacket with a wool scarf and cowboy boots—the fancy type made from some kind of reptile skin. I noticed something in one of his hands—a long, narrow, gift-wrapped box.

He was good-looking enough that it threw me a little. "May I help you?"

He just smiled at me as if waiting for me to recognize him. "Hi, Noel."

It took a moment, but I did. I recognized his eyes. He was Dylan Sparks, a boy I had been friends with in middle and high school. We were more than friends, actually; he was my first boyfriend, with all that that entailed.

"Dylan! I'm sorry. I didn't recognize you."

"Well, it's been a few years. I saw you were back in town so I thought I'd come by and say hi."

"Who told you I was back in town?"

"No one. I saw you at your father's funeral." He stood there for a moment, then said, "Am I interrupting something?"

"No, I was just reading."

"Of course you were," he said. He cocked his head. "Are you going to invite me in?"

"I'm sorry. Yes," I said, stepping back from the doorway.

He came inside and I shut the door behind him. "Have a seat."

"Thank you." He sat down on the couch next to the fireplace.

"Can I get you coffee or something?"

"No, I'm good."

I sat on the end of the couch facing him. "This is a little surreal."

He smiled. "Totally surreal. You look great, though. Time's been good to you."

"Thank you."

"I'm sorry about your father. He wasn't that old. How are you handling things?"

"I've been better."

"I bet," he said. "I brought you something." He handed me the box he'd been carrying. "I read that you should always send sweets after a death, to sweeten the bitterness of loss. I know how you used to like Fernwood's Mint Sandwiches."

I took the mints from him. "Thank you. I can't believe you remembered I like these. I haven't had one since I left."

"They're still good."

"And fattening."

"You didn't worry about that back then."

"There are a lot of things I didn't worry about back then."

"You and me both," he said. "What else is happening in your life?"

"Where do I begin? Pretty much everything is in commotion. I'm officially divorced."

"Is that a good or bad thing?"

"Jury's still out," I said. "All things considered, I'd rather be happily married. But I suppose it's better to live a bitter truth than a blissful lie. At least I keep telling myself that."

"I get it," he said. "Except I held on to the lie for as long as I could."

"You're divorced?"

He nodded. "Yeah. She left me. I kept telling myself it was just a phase she was going through and that she still loved me, she'd just forgotten. How's that for denial?" He exhaled as he shook his head. "In the end, the divorce was a formality. Truth was, she'd left us years before."

"Us?"

"I have a daughter. Alexis."

"How old is she?"

"Seven. Almost eight."

"I'm sorry. About the divorce."

"Me too. I liked her. I liked being married."

"You married Susan, right?"

He nodded. "Susan Tedesco. She was a dancer."

"I remember her. We took dance together. Only she stuck with it."

"At least she stuck with something."

"Was it painful?"

"The divorce?"

I nodded.

"Horribly. Rejection aside, I liked the idea of having a family. She saw settling down as settling for less; I saw it as a higher level of existence. You know my background. I don't take family or home for granted. Anyway, it's been five years now. Almost six." He looked at me. "How many years has it been since you left Utah?"

"It's been almost sixteen years."

He shook his head. "Has it really been that long?"

"Time flies when you're having fun."

"It also does when you're not." He looked into my eyes. "I've wondered about you. How you were doing. What you were doing."

"Making books," I said.

"I could have guessed that," he said. "I ran into your father a few years ago. We were at the same restaurant. He came over to talk to me. He told me you were working for some big-time New York publishing house. I wasn't surprised. Then he said, 'You were always good to Noel. I was glad you two were friends.' I asked him how you were doing personally. He said, 'She's married and seems happy. Other than that, I don't really know. She doesn't talk to me. I miss her.'"

"He probably just wanted you to think he cared," I said.

"He seemed sad when he said it." Dylan's forehead furrowed. "Why would he care if I thought he cared?"

I couldn't answer.

He clasped his hands together. "Anyway, how long will you be in Utah?"

"I'm not sure. I thought I was going back to work, but now . . . I guess not."

"What happened?"

"My supervisor called a few days ago to inform me that I no longer have a job."

He shook his head. "I'm sorry. When it rains it pours."

"The last person who said that to me took my job."

"Don't worry, I'm not after your job."

"So, what are you doing these days?" I asked. "Other than stalking me."

He grinned. "Mr. Mom. And I own a men's suit store."

"You sell suits?"

"High-end custom-tailored suits and tuxedoes for the discriminating male."

"I never would have guessed you'd end up doing that."

"What did you expect?"

"I thought you'd either be operating an oil rig in the middle of some ocean or have died saving hostages."

He smiled. "I know, right? One day I'm covered with plaster, putting up drywall for a future suit store, and the next thing I know, I'm selling suits."

"Another life parallel between us," I said. "One day I'm editing books, the next I'm selling them. I inherited my father's bookstore."

"It's like they say, 'When one door closes, another opens.'"

"More like when one door closes another one *falls* on you."

He laughed. "I think running a bookstore would be fun."

"We'll see. Culture hasn't been kind to independent bookstores. It feels a little like being handed the keys to a car as it goes over a cliff."

"It's not doing well?"

"Actually, my father's store is doing surprisingly well."

"I'm not surprised. I like your father's bookstore. Bobbooks. It's always busy when I'm there."

"Do you go there much?"

"Usually when I have a birthday or Mother's Day. They've got great candles."

"You go to the bookstore to buy candles?"

"Well, you don't sell coffee . . ."

I laughed. "No. My father never liked the idea of that. He didn't think coffee and books mixed. Not that candles do, either."

He leaned forward. "Speaking of which, we should get coffee sometime. Or maybe dinner?"

"I'd like that."

"How about Friday night?"

"You were serious."

"Why wouldn't I be?"

"I live in New York. *Sometime* usually means *never*."

"Well, I don't live in New York. So, Friday?"

"Friday would be great."

"Good. I just need to make sure that works with my mom."

"Your mom's coming with us?"

He grinned. "No. She's my sitter. She usually invites Alex over for sleepovers on the weekend anyway. She's her only grandchild, you know. She's kind of crazy about her."

"I can imagine."

"I'm off work at six. How about you?"

"I get off at five, so any time after six."

He stood. "Six thirty, then. I'll come straight from work."

I walked him to the door and opened it. He looked at me and smiled. "It's good seeing you, Noel. Have a good night."

"You too," I said.

As he was walking out I said, "Dylan."

He turned back.

"Thank you for coming by."

He smiled. "My pleasure."

I shut the door. At least I had one thing in my life to look forward to.

CHAPTER

fourteen

Quiet people have the loudest minds.

—Stephen Hawking

THURSDAY, NOVEMBER 5

Thursday morning I walked into Wendy's office. She was wearing a black bodysuit with a red sash, accentuating her hourglass figure.

"What's up, boss?"

Wendy looked up. "Are you really going to call me that?"

"I'm just respecting the arrangement."

"We need to start promoting our Black Friday book signings."

"You're still doing that?"

"You know how your father was. He loved his authors."

"Most of them," I said. "So, what do you need me to do?"

"Just make sure there are fliers in everyone's shopping bag."

"Where are they?"

"I left them on the front counter. Next to the register."

"I'll do it." I was about to leave when she said, "Oh, this

came for you." She handed me an envelope. The paper it was made from was textured and uneven, as if it were handmade. It was a light cream color.

"It's beautiful stationery," I said. "No return address. Who knows I'm here?"

"I suspect there are a few people who know you're in Utah."

"I mean at the bookstore."

"I haven't told anyone," Wendy said. "Probably just the IRS. They know everything."

I looked back down at the envelope. "I don't think the IRS has taken to using handmade cotton rag envelopes."

"You know stationery?"

"It's a passion of mine. There's a little stationery shop on Sixth Avenue. The owner makes his own paper and note-books."

"It's a lost art," Wendy said. "Your father loved it too."

I walked out to the front counter, then looked at the envelope again. After all the legal junk I'd been through with my divorce, I was just glad it wasn't a registered letter.

The postmark was from Salt Lake City and dated just the day before. I opened the envelope and pulled out the letter, which was written on the same paper. The handwriting was in a delicate, feminine script.

> *Dear Noel,*
> *Home is the port we seek when we weary of the turbulent sea. You have weathered enough storms, sweetheart. Welcome home.*
>
> *Tabula Rasa*

Tabula Rasa?

I was still looking down at the letter when Wendy emerged from the back. "I forgot to ask, were you planning on working late tonight?"

"I can."

"That would be good. Cyndee called in sick."

"I got it." She was about to go when I asked, "Do you know someone named Tabula Rasa?"

She looked at me quizzically. "You don't know what that is?"

I shook my head. "Not a clue."

"Tabula rasa," she said, carefully pronouncing the word, "isn't a *who*. It's a *what*. It's Latin for the theory that humans are born without mental content—so all we know is what we've been taught or experienced. Literally, the phrase means 'scraped tablet.' In other words, a blank slate. Why do you ask?"

I lifted the paper. "The letter I just got was signed 'Tabula Rasa.'"

"May I see it?"

I handed her the letter. She read it over, then handed it back. "Interesting pseudonym. I'd guess it was written by someone from the past who knows you're back in town and is hoping for a fresh start."

"Why would they write anonymously?"

She shrugged. "Best way to get read, right? Everyone loves a mystery. We've got two bookcases as proof. Any idea who might have written it?"

"Maybe," I said. "I guess I'll wait to see."

Wendy walked back to her office as I returned the letter to the envelope. I wondered what Dylan was up to.

CHAPTER

fifteen

You can make anything by writing.
—C. S. Lewis

FRIDAY, NOVEMBER 6

I first met Dylan when I was twelve, about a year and a half before my mother died. I immediately recognized that there was something different about him from the other boys my age. Even our schoolteachers seemed to treat him differently. I didn't learn until later that he was a foster child with a checkered past.

Dylan was the only child of two drug addicts. After he'd suffered years of neglect and abuse, his parents were reported to the state, and they gave up custody of him without protest—no doubt adding to the psychological damage that had already been done.

Dylan stayed with his maternal grandmother for a while, but, in his words, he was "too hot for her to handle." By "hot" he meant shoplifting, drinking, smoking, and running away. His grandmother was already in her eighties, and the two of them were an unlikely combination at best. Just four months later he was deemed a ward of the state.

Dylan was already in his third foster home when we met. I had two classes with him in seventh grade: algebra and English. I was immediately drawn to him. He wasn't hard to notice, as he naturally drew attention to himself, both good and bad. He was rebellious but also funny. Once he made our algebra teacher laugh, something the rest of us considered akin to parting the Red Sea.

Children always know who the "bad" kids in school are, and though Dylan was labeled as one, he wasn't mean. In fact, other than the occasional fight he'd get in, there was a surprising gentleness to his demeanor. Even my mother once commented that he was "such a polite young man."

Academically, Dylan was naturally gifted at math, something I had little interest in. On the other side, he hated English, which I excelled at. We quickly figured out that we could scratch each other's backs and began helping each other, which usually meant doing each other's homework. It was a match made in heaven. Or something like that.

The homework part was mostly a ruse to see each other. We began hanging out together all the time. He was the first boy I kissed. We began kissing a lot until his foster parents caught us and wouldn't allow me in his room anymore. We still kissed, just not at his house.

When my mother died, Dylan was the first one I told. I remember him holding me as I sobbed uncontrollably. Everything in my life changed after that. Some changes, like grief and anger, were immediate. Others were more gradual and less obvious. At least at first.

Although we remained friends into high school, it became evident that we were going in opposite directions. His foster parents, whom he had grown to like, asked to adopt him. That had a major impact on him. Where his biological parents had willingly given him up, here were two people fighting to keep him. He had finally found a home, and his days of rebellion were waning.

While Dylan was cleaning up his life, I was doing the opposite, wandering farther down a spiraling path of rebellion and self-destruction.

Despite Dylan's warnings, I started hanging out with some of the kids he used to hang out with. That's when I started pushing the limits, drinking and ditching classes. By my sophomore year, my grades fell from straight As to Ds and Fs.

My father was beside himself. Things came to a head one school day morning when he came home from the bookstore and caught me and my "friends" drinking in my room. He went ballistic.

That's the second time my world was uprooted. Three weeks later my father sent me away to a boarding school in Tucson, Arizona. To say I was unhappy was like saying the *Titanic* had had a rough crossing. I didn't talk to him from the moment I found out to the time I left, except for our final fight when I screamed at him that my mother's death was his fault. I remember that there were tears in his eyes.

The day before I left, Dylan came to say goodbye. It was the last time I saw him. He wrote me a few times in Arizona, but I never wrote back. I was cutting ties to everyone and everything that connected me to my old life, and Dylan was part of that. I vowed I would never go back to Utah.

CHAPTER

sixteen

A word after a word after a word is power.

—Margaret Atwood

Dylan picked me up for dinner at six thirty sharp. The restaurant he took me to was called Antica Sicilia. It was located in a small strip mall on Thirty-Ninth South next to a franchised hair salon.

It wasn't the kind of location you'd expect to find fine dining, but the owners and most of the staff were Sicilian immigrants, and the online reviews were remarkable. So was the wait. The small sitting area was full of people, and when a couple came in without a reservation requesting the next available table, the maître d' laughed. "*Porca miseria*. Maybe you try again next Wednesday."

Dylan had made reservations the night he came by my house, and we were quickly seated at a table near the open kitchen. One of the managers was also one of Dylan's clients, which didn't hurt. In fact, he came by our table to say hello. He was short, barely five feet tall, and wore an immaculate black suit with a sky-blue shirt open at the collar. Dylan introduced him to me as Salvatore.

"*Amico*," he said to Dylan. "You have found a new beauty."

He kissed Dylan on the cheeks, and then did the same to me. Dylan said, "This is my friend, Noel. She's from New York."

"Oh, New York. I love the city. It's been too long since I have been to the city. Thank you for joining us tonight."

"Piacere mia," I said, reaching the limit of my Italian.

His expression became animated. *"Mama mia,* she speaks *la bella lingua.* Mr. Dylan is a *buon amico.* I have sent you a bottle of Etna Rosso. Please, enjoy."

"Thank you," I said. After he left, I turned to Dylan. "That was nice."

"Salvatore's a good guy. I'm the only place in town he can get suits his size that weren't made for boys."

"You made that suit?"

"My tailors did."

"It's nice."

"Thank you. We do quality suits." He lifted his menu. "What would you like to eat?"

"What do you recommend?"

"Their signature dish is their 'flaming wheel of cheese' spaghetti carbonara. It's served tableside."

"That sounds good."

"Unless you're Charlie."

"Who's Charlie?"

"He's one of my employees. He has long hair that caught on fire while they were preparing it."

"Was he hurt?"

"No. I threw a glass of water on him. It made for an exciting meal." He looked back down at the menu. "I'll order some bruschetta as an appetizer. Do you like tomatoes?"

"Yes."

"And one caprese salad to share."

A waitress, one of the few non-Italians on the crew, took our order. Dylan filled my glass with wine, then his own.

"What should we toast?" he asked.

"How about books?" I said.

He lifted his glass. "To books." He took a sip of wine, then set the glass down. "Speaking of books, tell me about your job in New York."

"*Former* job," I said.

"Sorry. Your former employment."

"I *was* a senior editor for one of the big publishing houses."

"*Senior* editor. That sounds important."

"It's publishing. We get paid in titles, not paychecks."

"What do you do, correct spelling and grammar?"

"No. That's a different kind of editor."

"I didn't know there were different kinds of editors."

"Many," I said. "Just like there are different kinds of engineers. What you're describing is a copy editor. They tend to be a bit OCD. At least the good ones are. They're the kind of people who can't help but correct your grammar."

"We call them grammar Nazis," Dylan said. "They're annoying."

"They make my life a lot easier," I said.

"Then what kind of editor are you?"

"Senior editor is more of an all-purpose position. I'm kind of like a coach. I give my authors suggestions on their books and act as a liaison between them and the publishing house. Then, in my spare time, I also look for new talent, which means I'm reading constantly."

"That doesn't sound fun."

"You don't like reading?"

"Will it end our date if I say no?"

I cocked my head. "Is this a date?"

"One question at a time," he said. "No, I don't *hate* reading, per se. It's like anything else; once you're required to do it, it's not fun anymore. Basic human psychology."

"I'll forgive you, then," I said. "On account of basic human psychology. So, to the next question. Is this a date?"

"It's *dinner*," he said. "What skill set does it takes to be an editor?"

"Nice changeup," I said. "I'd say the two main qualities of being an editor are, first, you've got to love to read, and second, you can't want to make any money. That mostly sums it up."

"And you should probably love English," he added. "I got As in English because of you."

"Do you remember what they called me in school? Thesaurus Rex."

"That's a compliment."

"It's not when you're thirteen."

"Everything's upside down when you're thirteen."

"I've got news for you. Everything is still upside down."

He lifted his glass. "To upside down, then."

I clinked my glass to his and took a sip. "That's not bad wine."

"Salvatore's Sicilian. Bad wine is blasphemy. Or at least sacrilege." He poured a little more into my glass. "How's the bookstore doing?"

"It's been busy. I think the holiday season has officially begun for Bobbooks."

"Bobbooks," he repeated. "I love that name."

"That makes one of us."

He looked at me over the rim of his glass. "You don't like the name of your bookstore?"

"No. Never did."

"What's wrong with it?"

"I didn't say anything was wrong with it, I just said I don't like it. It's not my taste."

"What would you have named it?"

I held my hands up for emphasis. "It Was a Dark and Stormy Bookstore."

He looked at me blankly. "Explain it to me."

"If I have to explain, you still won't like it."

"Which is why it would make a bad name. Besides, it's way too long for a sign."

"That's your opinion," I said.

"No, I've bought signage—it's not cheap, and *Dark and Stormy* is a whole lot of letters, as opposed to *Bobbooks*, which is"—he stopped to count—"eight. Besides, the whole thing sounds gloomy."

"What's wrong with gloomy?"

"People read to get away from gloomy."

"Tell that to Stephen King."

"Stephen King's a writer, not a bookstore. Give me the name of a successful bookstore with a gloomy name."

"I'll give you three. Dearly Departed Books, Ohio. Dead End Books, New York. The Poisoned Pen in Scottsdale."

"Those are really names of bookstores?"

"They really are."

He looked down for a moment then said, "All right, apparently I know nothing about the book industry. I mean, I go to bookstores to buy coffee and candles. At least Bobbooks tells you what you're selling."

"Which isn't coffee or candles," I said.

We both ate for a moment then I asked, "What's the name of your store?"

He hesitated a beat then said, "It Was a Dark and Stormy Suit Store."

I laughed. "No, really."

"After all that I don't want to tell you."

"Please?"

"It's *Dylan's*. As in Dylan's custom suits for men."

"Dylan's," I repeated.

"I knew you wouldn't like it."

"No, I like it. It's . . . boutique-ish."

"Not sure if that's good, but I'll accept your pretended acceptance."

Ten minutes later our waitress returned with one of the chefs. He was pushing a stainless-steel cart carrying a large wheel of Parmesan cheese that was hollow in the middle and filled with spaghetti. He poured in a bowl of raw eggs and lit it on fire. He mixed the egg in with the pasta, then, after the flames were extinguished, served it up on our plates. A few minutes later Salvatore returned. *"Buon amici*, how is everything?"

"It's *buono*," Dylan said. He looked at me. "How is it?"

"It's delicious."

"Very good. *Tutto a posto*. Do not forget your *dolci*. It is on me."

We shared a cannoli for dessert, an Italian tube-shaped pastry that is deep fried and filled with sweetened ricotta cheese.

"You know, this dessert is almost two thousand years old," Dylan said.

"Hmm," I said. "It tastes fine to me."

He grinned.

I remembered what Dylan had told me about seeing my dad at an Italian restaurant. "Is this the restaurant where you saw my father?"

"Yes. He was sitting right over there." He pointed to a table two places away from us.

"Is that why you brought me here?"

"Nope. I brought you here because of the carbonara."

After dinner Dylan drove me home and walked me to my door.

"Would you like to come in?" I asked.

"I would, but I better get back to Alex. She's got ice-skating in the morning."

I took out my key and unlocked the door, then turned back to him. "That was really nice tonight. Thank you."

"Would you like to go out to dinner again?"

"No," I said. "I think we should go out on a *date* instead."

He smiled. "A date it is." I leaned forward and kissed him on the cheek. "Good night, Dylan."

"Good night."

I started to walk in, then turned back. "There have been a lot of storms in our lives, haven't there?"

He looked at me curiously. "Way too many."

I smiled. "Call me." I went inside. It was the best time I'd had in months.

CHAPTER

seventeen

You can never get a cup of tea large enough or
a book long enough to suit me.
—C. S. Lewis

SATURDAY, NOVEMBER 7

I woke up happy the next morning, the first time since I came to Utah. My dinner with Dylan had been unexpectedly pleasant. I hadn't had much luck with men as of late. If I were being completely truthful, that extended to women as well. Maybe I just didn't have much luck with people in general.

I ran my four miles around the park, showered and dressed, then went to the bookstore. Wendy wasn't expecting me, being Saturday, and she already had enough help, but I had nowhere else to be and the store was crowded, so I decided to stay.

Later that afternoon during a short break in traffic, I asked Wendy, "What do you think of selling coffee?"

"Is this like a Zen question, or does this have something to do with the bookstore?"

"I'll be more precise," I said. "What do you think of putting a café in our bookstore? Just look at that crummy coffee shop on the corner of Seventh. The Daily Grind. The only thing worse than their name is their coffee, but they've got a line that goes around the block every morning. Plus, I think it would class the place up, from bookseller to barista."

"Your father hated the idea."

"I know, but what do you think of it?"

"We would have to take out at least three bookcases to do it. What it comes down to is, books or coffee?"

"I think they can peacefully coexist," I said. "Where would we put it?"

"Here," she said, gesturing to the front counter. "It's the easiest access for customers and we could combine cash registers. And we'd have access to plumbing, since the bathroom is behind this wall."

I looked at her. "It sounds like you've thought this through."

"More than once. Just not with your father. He never wanted to talk about it."

"Fortunately, we're under new management."

Her expression turned. "You're half right."

That afternoon Wendy was up front putting out some new books when a woman walked up to me at the counter. "Excuse me. Where is your coffee?"

"We don't sell coffee."

"I mean, where's your café?"

"We don't have a café."

She looked at me like I had just told her the Earth was flat. "No café?"

"No, ma'am."

"Really? And you call yourself a bookstore." She turned and walked out.

"Did you hear that?" I asked Wendy.

"Books or coffee," she said.

CHAPTER

eighteen

Books are the blessed chloroform of the mind.

—James Payn

SUNDAY, NOVEMBER 8

Sunday was quiet. I had worked until closing on Saturday, so I was exhausted from the twelve-hour shift. I didn't run, but took a long bath and read most of the day. It snowed a little and I went out for coffee and to pick up some sushi, but that was about it. I thought of calling Dylan, but decided I'd wait for his call so that I didn't seem too eager. I'd seen *too eager* scare men away.

I went into work Monday. There weren't any customers in the store, and Wendy was changing the window display again.

"Looks like Saturday night was busy."

"It was," I said. "How does it compare to last year?"

"We're up twenty-one percent over this time last year. It's our third growth year in a row."

"That's good."

"Really good," she said. "We're on track for this to be our best season ever."

"Looks like Bob left a little too early."

"Robert," she said. "He hated it when people called him Bob."

"What does it matter?"

"It matters to me." She walked back to her office.

Grace came in a little after lunch.

"How are you today, Noel?"

"Well, thank you."

"How's your adjustment to Utah coming?"

"Slowly."

"Sometimes these things take time."

"Which I have plenty of. May I help you find something?"

"I'm looking for the book *Sapiens* by Yuval Noah Harari."

"I think we have that."

"You do. It's right over there." She walked directly to the book, took it from the shelf, then sat down in one of our armchairs to read. Twenty minutes later she brought the book over to the counter. "I'll take it."

"Very good." I scanned the book's barcode.

"Brava. You've learned how to use the cash register."

"Wendy taught me. I'm not much help if I can't sell books." I put the book in a sack along with a flyer for our Black Friday book signings. "Wendy told me you've bought a book every week for twenty years."

"That sounds about right."

"That's nearly a thousand books."

"I've purchased at least a thousand books," she said.

"Where do you keep them all?"

"I don't," she said. "I have a system. The great ones I keep in my library. The good ones I give to the public library. The bad ones I burn in my fireplace for wasting my time."

"You burn them?"

"I have a little ceremony in my living room fireplace. It's like my personal literary inquisition."

"How many books have you burned?"

"Many."

"How many books have you kept?"

"Few."

After she left, I went to Wendy's office. "Grace came in."

"Every Monday, one p.m.," she said, still focused on her computer. "Like clockwork. What did she buy this time?"

"*Sapiens.*"

"She'll like that. The *Guardian* listed it as one of the best brainy books of the decade."

"Is Grace smart?"

"Smart, rich, pretty . . ."

"Has she ever told you what she does with books she doesn't like?"

"She burns them." Wendy pressed a key on her keyboard, then looked back at me and smiled. "She's a book snob." She lifted an envelope from her desk. It was identical to the one I'd received before. "This came for you in the mail today. Looks like another letter from your secret admirer."

I took the envelope from her outstretched hand. "Thank you." I walked back out to the front of the store and opened it.

> *Dear Noel,*
> *The greatest story you will ever write in your life is*
> *your own, not with ink but with your daily actions*
> *and choices. Do not worry about perfection, it doesn't*
> *exist, it never has. All authors erase, all authors*
> *follow false paths that end up as crumpled paper in*
> *the trash basket. In the end it is not what you write*
> *but what you claim that is your story.*
>
> *Tabula Rasa*

Dylan called that night and asked me out for Wednesday. I almost thanked him for the letter.

CHAPTER

nineteen

Either write things worth reading, or do things worth the writing.

—Benjamin Franklin

WEDNESDAY, NOVEMBER 11

Wednesday evening Dylan picked me up a few minutes after I got home from work. We went out for Chinese at a restaurant called the Mandarin about fifteen minutes north of Salt Lake. The place was popular. Dylan told me that the wait was shorter than usual since it wasn't the weekend, but we still waited nearly half an hour to be seated.

We ordered family style so we could share everything. We got egg rolls, wonton soup, chicken fried rice, and a dish called Five Taste Shrimp. I was just glad to be with him again.

Dylan asked, "How old were we when we met? I'm thinking eleven or twelve."

"It was seventh grade, so a couple months before I turned twelve."

"Right," he said. "Your birthday's on Christmas."

"How sweet, you remembered."

"It doesn't take much of a memory. You were named after the day." He frowned. "I always thought that was unfortunate."

"That I was named Noel?"

He smiled. "No, I love your name. I meant having a birthday on Christmas."

"I know, right? I hated having my birthday on Christmas. The old ladies at Sunday school used to say, 'You're so lucky, you share a birthday with Jesus.'

"I always thought, *Oh yeah? You try sharing a birthday with Jesus.* Then when I was older I'd say, 'Actually, no one knows what day Jesus was born. The Bible doesn't tell us, and it's unlikely it was December twenty-fifth, since shepherds probably wouldn't be hanging out in the dead of winter just in case angels dropped by, and historians tell us that the celebration date was chosen by the emperor Constantine for political reasons, because it coincided with the existing pagan festivals."

"They must have been impressed."

"I think they were horrified. They would usually just walk away without saying anything."

"I would have been impressed," he said, taking a bite of egg roll. "How old were you when you said all that?"

"Nine."

He shook his head. "I definitely would have been impressed."

"My mom said I was a little girl with a big attitude."

"That's the Noel I remember."

"The thing about birthdays, it's the one day a year we get a little special attention. But when it falls on Christmas, forget about it. Most people viewed it as a two-in-one deal, so if I got a gift, they'd just say it was to cover both events."

Dylan laughed. "Your parents didn't celebrate your birthday?"

"No, my parents got it. We did an unbirthday party every June twenty-fifth, with a cake and candles."

"You made out a lot better than I did. I didn't know people celebrated birthdays until I was eleven."

"I'm sorry," I said. "You had it rough."

"For a while," he said.

Our waiter brought out our entrees, and we both filled our plates. Dylan waited until I had food in my mouth, then asked, "Do you remember the first time we met?"

I finished chewing and said, "It was your first day at school, and you were already in trouble for something. The teacher sent you to the principal's office."

Dylan grinned. "That sounds about right."

"I thought, *I could like this guy.*"

"That's really what you thought?"

"Actually, I thought, *He's really cute.* Then I thought, *I could like this guy.*"

"The first time I saw you, you were giving a book report in front of the class. I thought, *That girl is really pretty, and why does she talk like that?*"

"We already established that I talked like an adult."

"Thesaurus Rex," he said. "Then, after I got to know you and met your parents, I realized why you did. I thought they were the smartest people I had ever met."

"They were smart. I knew my father was smart because everyone said he was. When I was fifteen, I found out that he belonged to Mensa. I only knew because I saw a letter from them and asked what Mensa was. He told me so matter-of-factly that I didn't think much of it.

"I knew my mother was smart because I could ask her anything and she'd know the answer. And if she didn't, she'd stop what she was doing and look it up.

"Most parents get annoyed when their kids ask too many questions, but she encouraged me to be inquisitive." I smiled sadly. "After all these years I still miss her. Sometimes I find myself forgetting things about her. It scares me."

Dylan's expression turned somber. "I'll never forget that morning you called to tell me she had died. And then going to the funeral with my parents."

"That's when everything changed for me."

"It was just a few months after that that the Sparkses asked to adopt me." He frowned. "I think that was when things between us started to change."

"We were going in different directions. You found a family, and I lost mine. Then my dad shipped me off, and that ended us."

Dylan frowned. "I've never told anyone this, but the day you left, I went in my room and cried."

I looked at him. "I've never seen you cry."

"After what I went through as a kid, I never did. Except when you left."

"That's sweet," I said.

"Those were hard days."

"Those were hard days." After a minute, I said, "I think I need some wine. Would you like some?"

"No, thank you. But go ahead."

Dylan signaled our waiter, and I ordered a glass of Kung Fu Girl Riesling. After the waiter left, Dylan asked, "How long has your father had the bookstore?"

"As long as I remember."

"Was that always his dream? Selling books?"

"He loved his bookstore, but his real dream was to be a writer. Before my mother died, every month a group of wannabe writers gathered at our house. About six of them. They'd read parts of their books and critique one another's writing. Then some of the members would start drinking, and the evening would end with my father playing old Neil Young songs on his guitar."

"Classic," Dylan said. "Your father was pretty cool."

"No teenager thinks their father's cool," I said. "But he was smart and said funny things. Maybe he was cool."

"So why did you stop talking to each other?"

"I think it was my way of punishing him for my mother's death. Then exiling me."

Dylan's brow furrowed. "Why did you blame him for your mother's death?"

"I'd rather not get into that."

"I respect that," he said. "So, after high school, where did you go?"

"After graduation my father wanted me to come home, but I'd already been offered a scholarship to ASU, so I stayed in Arizona and went to college."

"What did you study?"

"English literature. My ultimate goal was to be a writer. I figured the best way to get there would be to get in with a big publisher. So I graduated from ASU with honors, and then a few months after that, I was accepted into the Columbia publishing program in New York. I kept getting farther away from Utah."

"And your father."

"And my father," I said. "He kept asking me to come back, even for a summer. I almost did, but then I met Marc. He was in the same publishing program at Columbia. He was already apprenticing as a literary agent at his godfather's New York firm. We got engaged after six months."

The waiter brought my glass of wine. I took a sip, then continued. "My father invited me to bring Marc back to Utah, but I didn't want to."

"Why not?"

"I don't know. Maybe because Marc came from a wealthy family and I didn't want him to see where we lived. So, my father flew out to meet him." I shook my head. "That was the final nail in the coffin of our relationship."

"So it didn't go well."

"It was a disaster. The three of us went out to dinner. Marc was acting really strange—because he was nervous, I guess—and he ended up drinking way too much. My father suggested to Marc that he not drink any more, and Marc exploded and said it wasn't any of my father's business. The scene turned ugly before my father apologized and de-escalated the situation. I remember going to the bathroom and crying.

"It was obvious that my father didn't approve of Marc, which I took as a personal affront. I told my dad to go back to Utah. He said, 'I'm sorry. I'm just looking out for you.' I said, 'I never asked you to.'

"He apologized again, then went to kiss me on the forehead, but I moved away from him. I'll never forget the pain on his face. He said, 'When you need me, I'll be there.' It was the last time I saw him.

"A week later I moved in with Marc, and a year later we got married. I didn't invite my father to my wedding."

Dylan looked at me thoughtfully. "Do you wish you had?"

"Sometimes."

"And the marriage . . ."

"Oh, that," I said. "I thought I had it all. We had a nice apartment in SoHo. I was loving my job, and Marc was doing well at his. I even considered sending him my father's book, but I never did."

"Why not?"

"Marc still didn't like him." I took a deep breath. "We'd been married about five years when I got pregnant. It was an accident. At first Marc said he was for it. Then I came home to find our apartment emptied. When I called Marc to ask what was going on, he told me he didn't want to be a father, he wasn't in love with me, and he was ready to move on. Just like that.

"After almost seven years of being together, he ended our marriage over the phone. I found out later that he had been having an affair with one of his authors for several years.

"Then I miscarried. I was too embarrassed or proud to call my father and tell him he was right, and that Marc had left me. He found out on his own and invited me to come back home. I just told him, 'I have a job, and New York is my home.'

"Then, about three weeks ago, I received a text from him

saying that he was dying of cancer and asking me to come home. I decided it was finally time to see him. He just waited too long to tell me."

Dylan asked, "Any regrets?"

I finished my glass of wine. "I'll let you know."

CHAPTER

twenty

The purpose of the writer is to keep civilization from destroying itself.

—Bernard Malamud

THURSDAY–FRIDAY, NOVEMBER 12–13

I didn't see Dylan for the next few days. There was some kind of Menswear Retailers show in Las Vegas that he needed to attend. It was held at one of the big resorts, and he vaguely hinted that the weather might be warm enough to swim or lay out. I wasn't sure if he meant that as an invitation or not, but I didn't take the bait. It was way too early to go on a trip together. Traveling is usually the best way to end a budding relationship.

I had a funny experience at the bookstore. A woman came in to return a book. Wendy had nicknames for some of our more *eccentric* customers, and this woman had definitely earned hers. Wendy called her the CURL—an acronym for "crazy ugly return lady." Even though Bobbooks had a lenient return policy, this woman pushed it to the extreme, basically using us as a library with benefits. Actually, not even a library would put up with what she attempted. I'm sure they'd revoke her card.

Nearly every month she would return a book for a full refund, claiming to have never read it. Wendy told me that she once bought a travel book on Hawaii. Three weeks later, when she returned it "unread," she was not only unseasonably tan but was wearing a lei and a flowered blouse.

Friday she brought in a copy of *The Girl on the Train* for a refund. It looked well read, as the spine was cracked.

"Is there something wrong with it?" I asked.

"I'll say. The writing was awful."

"It's been a very popular book," I said. "Let me see it." Instead of handing it to me, she set it on the counter, probably hoping I wouldn't examine it more closely. But even with it closed I could see that the pages were stained. I opened it to a massive grease mark that soaked through several dozen pages. I looked up at her for an explanation.

"Don't mind that," she said. "It's just the bookmark I was using."

"What kind of bookmark were you using?"

"Well, I was in a hurry and couldn't find any paper, so I used a strip of bacon."

"You used a strip of bacon as a bookmark?"

"Yes. It actually worked great."

I sighed. "You know I can't resell this."

"Can't you just return it to the publisher as defective?"

That afternoon I got another letter from Tabula Rasa. It was postmarked two days earlier.

> *Dear Noel,*
> *It's been written that "our greatest fear should not*
> *be of failure, but of succeeding at something that*
> *doesn't really matter." As you pursue your dreams,*
> *remember that when you turn the final page of life,*
> *what will matter most to you is only what can be held*
> *inside. Life's book is written on the heart.*
>
> *Tabula Rasa*

I thought back to Dylan's and my last dinner conversation and smiled.

I was happy when Dylan called me that night. There was a party that evening sponsored by one of the tuxedo makers but he had left early and gone back to his room to call me. We talked for nearly an hour.

"You could write a book about this place," he said. "It's like people just check out of their senses. They say what happens in Vegas stays in Vegas, but I think that just means your money."

I laughed. "I wish *you'd* come home."

"Are you missing me?"

"I am. And I'm lonely. And bored. When do you get back?"

"I'll be home late Monday night."

"Can I see you then?"

"It's pretty late. I'll have to take care of Alex."

"Then Tuesday?"

He groaned. "I'm sorry. More fatherhood. After work I've got a school meeting with Alex's teacher. How about Wednesday?"

"I'll take what I can get."

"I'm sorry. I miss you too. The life of a single father's a little hectic."

"I get it. Then I'll see you Wednesday."

"Wednesday it is. Bye."

I hung up the phone and lay back on the couch. He was just being a good father. Of all people, I should appreciate that. Then why did it upset me?

CHAPTER

twenty–one

I went for years not finishing anything.
Because, of course, when you finish something you can be judged.

—Erica Jong

MONDAY, NOVEMBER 16

Monday afternoon Grace showed up at the store at her usual time. She grabbed a book and carried it up to the counter. *Go Set a Watchman* by Harper Lee.

"I read that this was one of the most anticipated books in history," she said.

"It's Lee's first book since *To Kill a Mockingbird*," I said.

"Fifty-five years of bottled anticipation," Grace said.

As I scanned the book for payment I said, "It came out last July. I'm surprised you're just reading it now."

"I was letting the hype die down a bit so I could judge for myself if it's any good." She handed me her credit card. "You know, there was a lot of controversy surrounding *Mockingbird*."

"Because it's about racism?"

"There was that, of course. But many critics didn't believe Lee wrote it."

"Who did they think wrote it?"

"Lee's childhood friend, Truman Capote. You must admit that it's an unlikely coincidence that two world-famous authors grew up next door to each other. Then, after the book became a huge bestseller, Ms. Lee added to the controversy by avoiding all publicity—for herself and her book. It was as if she were afraid to talk about it."

"No one would do that today," I said.

"No, they wouldn't. These days, people can't seem to get enough attention." She looked into my face. "It must be interesting for you to see what's happening on the other end of the pipe."

"What do you mean?"

"Back in New York, you cobble together a book in some isolated inner sanctum, drop it into the distribution tube, and this is where it pops out. It's like a general's staff waging war miles behind the battlefield. Bookstores are the front line. It's where books live or die."

I liked her observation. "You're right. There was a publisher at one of the houses that made all her senior editors work in a bookstore for at least a month before they were promoted."

"Smart woman," Grace said. "Maybe that's why your father wrote so well."

"Why is that?"

She gestured to the store around us. "He was on the front lines."

Her comment sparked a memory. "Can I ask you something? What was the book you put in my father's casket?"

She looked at me for a moment, then said, "*May*, dear. *May* I ask you something." Without answering me she turned and walked out of the store.

CHAPTER

twenty–two

To survive, you must tell stories.

—Umberto Eco

TUESDAY, NOVEMBER 17

Tuesday afternoon I received my fourth letter. I checked the envelope's postmark. It was the same as the others, which perplexed me a little, as Dylan had been in Las Vegas.

Dear Noel,
Two thoughts on living a meaningful life: First, live
big. Expect the world and the abundance of it. It
is the only way to claim the full measure of your
creation. What we expect of life is all it can be.

Second, live small. In the end (and beginning and
middle), it's the little things that add up to create the
big. The vast lake of your life experience is fed by a
small but constant stream.

If these two counsels seem contradictory, so be it. Life itself is an irony.

On life's journey, avoid shortcuts to the important destinations. They usually lead to cliffs.

Live big, but do not create expectations of yourself that can't be reached. Remember, no one's perfect. Even God made broccoli.

Tabula Rasa

CHAPTER

twenty–three

I must say I find television very educational. The minute somebody turns it on, I go into the library and read a good book.

—Groucho Marx

WEDNESDAY, NOVEMBER 18

It had been nearly a week since I had seen Dylan. I called him from work and suggested that instead of going out we make pizza at my house and watch a movie. He liked the idea.

"If you get the DVD, I'll pick up the ingredients on the way home," I said. "What do you like on your pizza?"

"The usual. Pepperoni. Sausage. Ham."

"That's all meat," I said. "What about vegetables?"

"Mushrooms, olives, green peppers."

"How about broccoli?"

"Broccoli on pizza? I think not."

"What about broccoli in general?"

"Do you mean do I like it?"

"Yes."

"If I were sentenced to death, I probably wouldn't include it in my last meal."

"Fair enough," I said.

Dylan arrived around seven, nearly a half hour late.

"I'm so sorry," he said. "The babysitter was late, and Alex wasn't happy I was leaving. She gets upset when I've been gone."

"I understand. You're her only parent."

We made two small pizzas. Mine was a simple margherita with basil, tomato, and mozzarella. Dylan's had everything on it that I had bought. We followed dinner with a vanilla-orange gelato that Dylan had picked up with a DVD on the way to my house.

He had chosen the movie *Everest*, based on the ill-fated 1996 expedition that claimed eight lives. I had read the Jon Krakauer book *Into Thin Air*, about the same tragic expedition. The book was better than the movie, but the movie was good, and the book gave me deeper context. It was only the second time since I came back that I had watched television, demonstrating how successfully my father had ingrained in me the evils of the medium.

"I don't think I'll ever climb Everest," I said, taking the DVD from the player.

"And I will not climb it with you," Dylan said.

I grinned. "Thanks for your support." As I turned back to him I had an idea. "Hey, can you help me with something?"

"Absolutely."

"My father has a safe in his closet. He left me the combination, but I haven't been able to open it. Think you can?"

"I can give it a try."

I led him to the safe, then retrieved the paper with the combination and handed it to him while he got down on his knees in front of it. I sat on the floor behind him.

"What's in it?"

"I don't know. My father's lawyer said it contained some of his most valuable possessions."

"Then let's open it." He looked over the combination. "Your father's writing is kind of hard to read. Especially in the dark."

"He was famous for his bad handwriting."

He handed me back the paper. "Here, you read it to me."

I read the numbers as he dialed them in. After four tries he shook his head. "Are you sure that's the right combination?"

"It's the only one I have."

He turned back toward the safe. "You might have to hire someone to open it." Dylan got back to his feet, then checked his watch. "I'm sorry. I should probably be getting home." We walked back out to the living room. As Dylan put on his coat he asked, "What are you doing for Thanksgiving?"

"I don't have any plans."

"Then you can spend it with us."

"You and Alex?"

"And my parents. We have dinner at their house every year. They would love to have you over. You know my mom can cook."

"I'd like that. Thank you."

"Alex will be especially happy. It was her idea to invite you."

I raised my eyebrows. "Oh, it wasn't yours?"

"No. I tried to talk her out of it, but she was pretty stubborn."

"Smart girl. What can I bring?"

"How about a book for my mom?"

"That's not what I meant. I'd be happy to bring a book, but what food can I bring?"

"I don't think my mom accepts contributions to her meal. She's picky that way. I can ask. She might not be too upset."

"I don't want to upset her," I said. "I'll just bring a book. What time do you eat?"

"Usually around two. Do you have plans before that?"

"Not really. I'll probably just go for a run."

"Well, if you're up to it, it's Alex's and my tradition to pick out a Christmas tree. You're welcome to join us."

"That sounds fun. What time?"

"A little before noon. That will give us time to put it up and decorate it then get over to my parents."

"That will be great," I said.

"Great," he echoed. "I'll pick you up around eleven thirty. Dress warm." We lightly kissed, then I watched him walk to his truck. I waved once more, then shut the door.

I was looking forward to seeing Dylan's parents again. I had once spent a fair amount of time at their house. Charlotte was a strong, southern matriarch, a housewife who spent much of her time engaged in charitable causes. You could say that Dylan was one of them. After several other foster homes had given up on him, Charlotte and Dylan's father, Stratton, stepped in as foster parents, eventually winning him over.

It wasn't surprising that Charlotte showed such interest in me after my mother's death. I suppose that I, too, was a cause. Even after I left Utah, she sent me birthday-Christmas cards and occasional letters, which I never reciprocated or thanked her for. I hoped she'd forgotten that I'd been so rude.

CHAPTER

twenty–four

FRIDAY, NOVEMBER 20

Dear Noel,
Life, to be fully lived, must be lived free. The key to
freedom is forgiveness. Forgiveness is a virtue often
misunderstood. It is not to close our eyes to wrongs,
rather to truly open them and see the wider picture.
Forgiveness is release—to unlock the cage of another's
folly to set ourselves free.

To not forgive is to chain oneself to people
and circumstances of the past. In doing so, our
past becomes our future. This bears repeating. By
chaining ourselves to actions of the past, our past
becomes our future.

Let the past go, Noel. In the chess game of life,
the past makes a good bishop but a poor king. We
may take counsel from the past, but we should not be
ruled by it. One cannot ride a horse backward and
still hold its reins.

Tabula Rasa

CHAPTER

twenty–five

Books are the best type of the influence of the past.

—Ralph Waldo Emerson

MONDAY, NOVEMBER 23

For the first time since I'd helped Grace, we didn't have the book she was looking for: *Kissinger's Shadow*, a nonfiction work on the American statesman. We had brought in five copies and they were already sold. It was a good example of just how eclectic Grace's taste in books was: from French hors d'oeuvres to global politics.

"Don't worry yourself about it," she said. "Wendy can order it."

"I hate for you to leave without a book."

"Not to worry," she said. "It won't be the first time." She smiled. "I'm sure I can find something to read at home."

"If you haven't burned them," I said.

"If they were burn-worthy, I wouldn't waste my time reading them again," she said. "Oh, you might want to see what's going on in the back of the store. Near the crime novels."

"What's going on?"

"It's better if you just go on back."

As she left the store I walked to the back corner, where I found a woman slightly stooped with her back to me. She was holding what looked like a jar, tipped on its side.

"May I help you?" I asked.

The woman spun around. Her face was beet red. It wasn't a jar in her hands but an urn.

"Oh, you caught me," she said.

I was still perplexed by what I was looking at. "What did I catch?"

"My father used to love crime novels, so I was just spreading his ashes where he was most happy."

I looked at the pile of ashes that was already on the floor. "No."

"Just a—"

"No. Take your . . . father . . . and leave."

She scooped what ashes she could back in the urn. "It's my father," she said.

"Exactly."

Near the front door she said, "I'm not ever coming back."

"I hope that's a promise," I replied.

After she was gone I went and told Wendy. She just shook her head. "Really? People are always trying to dump ashes in Disneyland, but in a bookstore?"

"They dump ashes in Disneyland?"

"Pirates of the Caribbean," Wendy said. "They have cameras everywhere. Did she get him all up?"

"No. The ashes stained the carpet."

Wendy sighed. "Someone's going to have to vacuum up her father."

CHAPTER

twenty–six

I write to discover what I know.

—Flannery O'Connor

TUESDAY, NOVEMBER 24

The next day was busy; people were buying gifts as they prepared for Thanksgiving. I didn't know how much money the bookstore was making, but I figured it was probably a lot.

Also, Tabula Rasa delivered as expected.

Dear Noel,
As you are confronted each day by new ideas
and propositions, do not forget to think. View
each matter of importance from as many angles
as is practical. Do not be swift to throw in with
the current of mainstream thought or waves of
indoctrination. Avoid anyone who offers to do

your thinking for you. The masses follow a media shepherd.

Many mistake knowledge for wisdom. They are not the same thing. A cupboard full of ingredients is not a meal. It's how knowledge is applied to real life that counts as wisdom. The world is overflowing with educated idiots, people who spout what they do not understand, profess what they cannot defend, advocate what they do not live, and claim what they do not own. Do not be over-arrogant in your knowledge. No one is always right, and everyone is sometimes wrong.

Tabula Rasa

CHAPTER

twenty-seven

A good writer possesses not only his own spirit but also the spirit of his friends.

—Friedrich Nietzche

THURSDAY, NOVEMBER 26

Thanksgiving morning, Dylan rang the doorbell a few minutes before eleven thirty. I grabbed my purse and opened the door. Dylan was standing there with his daughter, Alexis, holding her hand. It was the first time I'd seen her.

Alexis looked small for a seven-year-old. She was bundled up in a pink parka with a pink scarf and baby-blue knit mittens with a matching stocking cap, her blond hair peeking out like weeds growing from beneath a porch deck. She was a pretty little girl, which wasn't surprising, considering her parents' genes.

"I'm Alexis," she said to me. "But my dad calls me Alex. Unless he's mad at me."

"May I call you Alex too?"

She nodded. "We're going to get a Christmas tree."

"That sounds fun. Is it okay if I come with you?"

"My dad says it's okay."

"Then it must be okay." I looked up at Dylan.

"You heard it," he said.

We walked out to Dylan's truck. He opened the passenger side door, lifted Alexis into the back, then helped me in. He then went around to the driver's side and climbed in. "Who's ready to buy a Christmas tree?" he asked.

Alexis screamed, "Me!"

"Me too," I said.

"All right, let the Christmas tree expedition begin."

We drove to a tree lot situated in the parking lot of a nearby Walmart. The lot wasn't busy, and we walked up and down the rows of trees alone.

"Is there a particular kind of tree you're looking for?" I asked.

"The Fraser fir is a classic. As is the Douglas fir. They both hold their needles well, but the Fraser smells more like Christmas."

"I didn't know you were a Christmas tree connoisseur. What does Christmas smell like?"

"Magic."

I grinned. "What does magic smell like?"

"Childhood."

I stopped at a tree that looked perfectly shaped. "What kind of tree is this?"

"I have no idea. I actually just read up on trees this morning to impress you."

"Look, Dad. It's the right shape," Alexis said. "It's a cone."

Dylan said, "I taught Alex that there's a geometric formula for selecting the right tree. When she was four, I taught her to look for an isosceles triangle. A year later she graduated to the concept of a cone. The ideal tree is one where the apex is perpendicular to the base. Or, in layman's terms, a cone whose altitude intersects the plane of the circle at the circle's center."

"I think you just took all the fun out of Christmas," I said.

"Math, *especially* geometry, is all about fun."

"You are a geek," I said. "But fun."

"It's a package deal."

We selected a near-geometrically perfect Fraser fir, and the guy at the lot trimmed the bottom and put it in the back of Dylan's truck. Then we drove to his house to decorate it.

Dylan's home was only about four miles southeast from mine in the Millcreek area of Salt Lake in the foothills of the mountains, which is why he had so much more snow than I did; his roof was capped with at least two feet. It was a beautiful home with a river rock façade and a creek bed, currently frozen, cutting through the front yard.

"What a beautiful home," I said.

"Thanks. Susan found it. It was a bit of a fixer-upper, but I was doing remodeling work at the time, so it worked out perfectly."

Dylan backed his truck into the driveway, which looked like it had been carved out of a thick sheet of snow, the banks on each side more than three feet high. He took the keys from the truck and handed them to me. "If you take Alex and open the front door, I'll get the tree."

I took Alexis's hand, and we walked up the shoveled walk to the front porch. I unlocked and opened the door, then waited as Dylan lifted the tree out of the truck's bed. I held the door for him as he carried it in, then shut it after him.

The home was warm and welcoming, decorated with sleek modern decor. Looking around the room, I realized that I really didn't know the adult Dylan. He was wild and unkempt as a boy, and I never suspected he would grow to be so organized and, frankly, clean. Cleaner than me.

He had already brought up boxes of decorations and strands of lights, which were laid out along one side of the room. He dropped the tree into a stand in one of the corners of the front room.

"You've got a system here," I said.

"That's the way we roll around here. It's all about systems. Especially when you're a single dad. Would you hold the tree while I clamp it in?"

"Of course."

I held the tree steady while Dylan got down under the boughs and screwed the stand's bolts into the trunk.

"That should do," he said, getting up off his knees. "Now the lights."

I helped him string up the lights, which were LED but retro in design, brightly colored and round as ping-pong balls.

"Alex," he called. "I need your help."

Alex walked into the room. "What, Daddy?"

"You know your job."

"Okay." She looked at me. "I always plug it in. I'm good at it."

"I can't wait to see," I said.

Dylan handed Alex the end of the cord. She got down on her knees and plugged it into the socket. The tree glowed. Alex clapped, and Dylan and I quickly joined in.

"Well done," he said. "No one can plug a tree in like Alex."

Alex smiled. "No one, Daddy."

"What comes next in your system?" I asked.

"Hanging the tinsel," he said. "Then the ornaments."

"I can do that." Then, looking at Alexis, I added, "I mean, *we* can do that."

"Would you like some hot cocoa?"

"I would love some."

"I don't need to ask you, beautiful girl," he said to Alexis. "Extra mallows."

"Extra mallows," she said.

Alex and I began draping the tinsel on the tree while Dylan disappeared into the kitchen. A few minutes later he came out with three mugs on a tray with peppermint sticks and steam rising above their tops. He set the tray down on the coffee table then handed me one of the mugs. There was writing on it.

Those who believe in telekinetics, raise my hand.
Kurt Vonnegut

"Nice mug," I said. "You know, my father was a huge Vonnegut fan."

"I might have bought that mug at your bookstore."

"I wouldn't be surprised." I took a sip of cocoa.

"You sell coffee mugs but not coffee," he said. "Go figure."

"The book world defies explanation."

CHAPTER

twenty–eight

As a writer you should not judge. You should understand.

—Ernest Hemingway

A lexis and I finished hanging the ornaments, and then she went up to her room while Dylan and I sat in front of the tree sipping our cocoa.

"May I ask a personal question?"

Dylan shrugged. "You can ask."

I looked up to make sure Alex wasn't listening, then asked softly, "Why didn't Susan end up with Alex? I mean, it's usually the way it goes."

Dylan frowned and set down his cup. "She didn't want her. Susan got in with a group of friends who convinced her that family and home took away her freedom. She saw the house, Alex, and me as chains. Or at least anchors."

"That's sad."

"It's true. At least in part. I agree with her premise, but not her conclusion. Home *is* an anchor. But that's not a bad thing. Anchors are valuable. The sea is turbulent; it's a gift to hold ground. People talk about 'freedom' as if life were measured by mileage. It's not."

"What is life measured by?"

"Matters of consequence, like being a good human."

"For a mathematician you're surprisingly poetic."

"Math is poetry," he replied.

"I think I agree with you." I took another drink of cocoa, then leaned back into the soft couch. "It really is a pretty tree."

"Thank you."

"Where do you get your ornaments?"

"The blue and red ones from Target. The unique ones from all over. It's Alex's and my tradition. We buy a new ornament every year. We still haven't gotten this year's yet."

"How long have you had this tradition?"

"Four years. We started the year Susie left. Alex and I were at the mall shopping, and she kept crying for her mommy. I was looking for something to cheer her up. An ornament did it." He grinned. "And ice cream."

"Ice cream is powerful," I said.

"Very powerful. And now I'm getting hungry." He looked down at his watch. "It's almost time for dinner."

"What time are we supposed to be at your parents' place?"

"In fifteen minutes. We should leave." He stood and shouted to Alexis. "Alex. Time to go to Meemaw's."

"I'm coming."

I also stood. "I still feel bad not helping your mother cook."

"Guilt without cause. She would throw you out of her

kitchen like spoiled milk. Or, she'd let you help but then never invite you back."

"Really?"

"I've seen it happen. It's her domain. Dad and I grew up with 'Get out of my kitchen.'" Dylan turned toward the stairs. "Alexis. It's time to go. Now."

"I'm coming!" A minute later she came down the stairs.

"Where were you?" Dylan asked.

Alexis was obviously embarrassed and whispered to Dylan forcefully, "I was in the bathroom."

Dylan winked at me. "Sorry."

Dylan's parents lived in the same wood-shingled box of a house they had when he and I went to school together. It was about two miles from where I lived, just north of the park a few blocks. Like my home, theirs was in an older neighborhood that had gone through gentrification and had become a yuppie paradise, surrounded by remodeled homes and expensive cars.

Seeing the old place brought back memories as thick as moths around a country porchlight.

"It's been a while," Dylan said. "Do you remember it?"

"Like my own house. It hasn't changed much."

He took my hand. "Neither have my parents."

CHAPTER

twenty–nine

Wanting to meet an author because you like his work is like wanting to meet a duck because you like pâté.

—*Margaret Atwood*

Stratton and Charlotte Sparks were as southern as boiled peanuts. Stratton called her "Sweet Pea," and Charlotte called him "Honey Bun" or, more often, "Strat." They were transplants from Huntsville, Alabama. They had met when they were twelve, married at nineteen, and then come out to Utah when Stratton was stationed as a JAG at Hill Air Force Base in Ogden.

Unable to have children of their own, they registered with Children's Services as foster parents, hoping to someday adopt one of the children they were helping. That child was Dylan.

About the time Dylan came along, Stratton had just left the military and gotten a job downtown at a large Salt Lake legal firm. That's when they moved to the Sugar House area, a chain of events that helped Dylan's and my paths to cross.

They were a big part of my childhood at a critical time in my life. I don't remember Stratton being around much in those days—probably because of his new job—but it was always pleasant when he was. I once told Dylan that his father scared me. Dylan just laughed. "I know," he said. "He looks scary, but he's about as mean as a cotton boll."

Stratton was quiet, with a surprisingly wry sense of humor. I don't think I'd ever been with him when he hadn't told at least one joke (or at least something that resembled one).

Charlotte was strong-willed, proper, and beautiful. And an excellent cook. She'd brought her southern cuisine with her to Utah, and she gave me my first taste of cheese and grits, black-eyed peas, and collard greens, something most Utahns will never experience.

"Is anyone else eating with us?" I asked as we pulled into the driveway.

"Just us and the folks." Dylan parked his truck and we walked through the side door into the kitchen. "We're here," Dylan announced as we walked in.

"Where's my princess?" Stratton shouted from an unseen room.

"Pawpaw!" Alexis shouted, running off to find her grandfather.

With the exception of some new wallpaper and carpet, the interior of the house hadn't changed much since I'd last been there. From the side entryway, I could see the dining room table. It was beautifully arranged with a long ivory tablecloth and a centerpiece of autumn-colored flowers: orange roses; mums of yellow, bronze, and rust; and green huckleberry. Two unlit orange tapered candles rose from the center.

The table was set for five with floral and gold-embossed

china, crystal goblets, and silverware on linen napkins. Mrs. Sparks ascribed to a southern formality that few take time for in the bustle of modern life.

Dylan led me into the kitchen, where his mother was leaning over the stove stirring something in a pot. Charlotte looked older than I remembered, but was still very pretty, with curled yellow hair. She was wearing a flowery apron over a long mint-and-ivory dress with a matching sash and a lace hem. A symphony of aromas wafted through the room.

"The house smells amazing, Mom. As usual."

"Thanks, honey," she said, kissing him on the cheek. "It's about time y'all got here." She turned to me, her expression growing even more animated. "No-el," she drawled. "Just look at you. You've grown into such a beautiful woman. I was so happy to hear Dylan say you would be joining us today."

"Thank you, Mrs. Sparks. I've really been looking forward to this."

"And honey, I'm just so sorry to hear about your dear father. He was such a good man."

"Thank you, ma'am."

"Call me Charlotte, honey. Did y'all get your Christmas tree put up?"

"Yes, we did," Dylan said.

"It's a tradition of his," Charlotte said to me. "We can't have too many traditions. Tradition is the foundation that you build a family on."

"I brought something for you," I said. I handed her the wrapped book.

"Oh, honey. You didn't need to bring me anything."

"It's just a book."

She set it aside. "Bless you. I'll enjoy opening it after supper."

"Is there something I can do to help?"

"No, we're just about ready. Wait, there is one thing." She turned to Dylan. "Son, would you pour the sweet tea and light the candles? You can leave the pitcher on the table."

"I'm on it."

"You're a dear. The pitcher's in the fridge."

She turned back to me. "There's hot crawfish dip in the living room you can nibble on. And I got you some of those mint sandwiches you were so fond of."

"Thank you."

"Now you just go out and sit with Strat and relax while I finish things up."

"Go on," Dylan said. "I'll be right there. Just don't eat it all."

"I'll try to restrain myself."

I went into the front room. Dylan's father was sitting at the piano with Alexis, teaching her how to play something. He turned around as I walked in then stood to greet me. He looked exactly the same as I remembered, except he was shorter and his hair had gone completely gray. His smile was as big as I remembered. "Noel Book. It's been a year of Sundays."

"Actually, longer," I said. "Happy Thanksgiving."

"And a Happy Thanksgiving to you. Charlotte and I were so looking forward to having you join us."

"It's all my pleasure."

"Not all yours," he said.

"Pawpaw's teaching me a song on the piano," Alexis said. "'I Want a Hippopotamus for Christmas.'"

"Do you know what a hippopotamus is?" I asked.

She looked at me like I was a fool. "Of course. It's a short elephant without a trunk."

"That's the best definition I've ever heard," I said. I turned to Stratton. "I didn't know you played the piano."

"Not like I used to. During law school I played at a bar on weekends for spending money. Now I just do a hymn now and then, or a Billy Joel song. I used to love to play that 'Rootbeer Rag' before my arthritis flared up."

Alexis pounded at the keys until Dylan walked in. "Hey, Dad."

"Hi, Son. Alex says you got your tree up."

"Yes, we did. Did you get a haircut?"

"No. I pretty much got them all cut."

Dylan grimaced. "I walked into that." He turned to me. "Did you try the dip yet?"

"Not yet."

"Well, it's not going to eat itself." He walked over and got a little plastic plate and scooped some dip onto it along with cubes of French bread and handed it to me. Then he did the same for himself. "Nothing like southern cooking."

Stratton replied, "Only thing better than southern cooking is a southern woman."

"I heard that," Charlotte shouted from the kitchen.

Stratton winked at us. "I hoped she would."

About five minutes later Charlotte walked into the living room. "Dinner's on."

"All right," Stratton said. "You heard the woman. Let's eat."

We sat around the oval table; Stratton on one end, Dylan on the other, with Alexis and me at his sides. I was about to start putting food on my plate when Dylan reached over and took my hand. "Grace," he said.

"I'll offer grace," Stratton said. "Dear God, thank you for this bounty and this day to give thanks. We are grateful to live in a free country and to have each other. We are grateful today that Miss Noel has joined us and ask your blessings to be upon her at this sorrowful time of loss. We praise thee and say thanks for all we have, in His name we praise, Amen."

"Amen," I said. I couldn't remember the last time I had prayed.

Stratton rose and began to carve the turkey.

"Dylan says that you've been living in New York City," Charlotte said.

"Yes, ma'am. Charlotte."

"What do you do there?"

"I was an editor for a publishing house."

"So you work with authors?"

"Yes, ma'am."

"Any that I may know?"

"Kiel Taylor, Debbie Rasmussen, W. W. Spooner, Jerica Bradley."

"You've met Jerica Bradley?" she exclaimed.

"I work with her. I help edit her books."

"You work with *the* Jerica Bradley? You know, I just love her books. I've read every one of them. She must be just a delight to work with."

I bit my lip.

She leaned forward. "Tell me, what's she like? In real life."

I carefully considered my response, as I'm not one to burst bubbles. "She's very talented."

"Isn't that God's truth. The next time you see her, please tell her that I'm her biggest fan and to keep up the good work."

"I would be happy to."

"Will you be staying in Utah for a while?" Stratton asked.

"At least until Christmas. I'm still figuring things out."

"I hope you don't go away," Alexis said.

"Thank you. That's very sweet."

"Noel has inherited her father's bookstore," Dylan said.

"Bobbooks," Stratton said. "Over on Ninth and Ninth. I like that bookstore. It has a very classic feel to it. Reminds me of a little bookstore in Huntsville I used to patronize."

"Noel doesn't like the name," Dylan said.

I kicked him under the table.

"Wasn't your father's name Bob?" Stratton asked.

"Robert," I said. "He never liked the name Bob."

"But he named his bookstore Bob's books," Stratton observed.

"It's actually Bobbooks. It's kind of a made-up word. He liked the sound of it. Originally, he was going to name it Book's Books, but he didn't think people would get it."

"Noel wants to change the name," Dylan said. "She has an idea for a better one." He looked at me. "Go ahead, tell them."

I resisted kicking him again.

"What would you change it to?" Charlotte asked.

Now I really wanted to kick him. "Well, it's a little unusual." I swallowed. "It Was a Dark and Stormy Bookstore."

Both Charlotte and Stratton looked at me blankly. Finally, Charlotte said, "Isn't that interesting. You always did march to your own drummer, didn't you? Good for you."

I glared at Dylan. I could tell he was dying to laugh.

I was glad when the conversation changed to something other than me, the bookstore, or anything else of personal embarrassment. At one point, Charlotte went off talking about Stratton's sister who, three years earlier, at the ripe age of sixty-two, left her husband to become a country singer. "She's no spring chicken," Charlotte said. "It's no surprise her star never rose."

"No," Stratton added. "That was a fool thing. But not all surprising. Her biscuit was never quite done in the middle."

"God bless her," Charlotte said.

Stratton turned to me. "So you're a book editor?"

I nodded. "I was."

"Then you might appreciate this. A woman was sitting at her deceased husband's funeral when a man leaned forward and said, 'Do you mind if I say a word?'

"The woman replied, 'No, you go right ahead.' The man stood up, cleared his throat, and said, 'Plethora.' Then he sat back down.

"'Thank you,' the woman said. 'That means a lot.'"

Dylan laughed. Charlotte wasn't pleased. "Strat," she said. "What in the world were you thinking? Noel just lost her daddy."

Stratton turned to me. "I guess I wasn't thinking. I'm very sorry."

"That's okay," I said. "My dad would have liked that."

The meal was authentically southern. There was bacon-wrapped turkey with cornbread dressing, biscuits, creamy corn pudding, crunchy green bean casserole, and sweet potato casserole with plenty of sweet tea to wash it all down. After dinner Charlotte served coffee and pecan pie.

I had just started on my pie when Stratton asked, "Noel, do you have a place in New York?"

"I did when I left. I was living with a roommate, but I'm being kicked out next week. So, technically, I'm homeless."

"She has a home here," Dylan said. "She inherited her father's place."

"What about your job?"

"I was kind of kicked out of that too."

"Looks like the Lord has other plans for you," Charlotte said.

"Well," Stratton said, "I hope you end up back here. It's a nice place to raise a family."

Stratton brought out a cigar and was about to light up when Charlotte said, "Not here, Strat. We have guests."

It was a wonderful meal. Not just the food, which was perfect, but the joy of it all—the laughter and stories and familiarity; a magical quality of family that permeated every moment. It felt like home.

CHAPTER

thirty

I never knew how to worship until I knew how to love.

—Henry Ward Beecher

After dinner Dylan and I went into the kitchen to clean up. Charlotte tried to help, but we barred her from the room, so she went to the living room with Alexis and Stratton. After we finished the dishes, Dylan and I found his mother.

"Mom, would you mind watching Alex for a little bit? I'm going to drive Noel home."

"Of course, dear. Take your time. There's no hurry."

"Thank you for dinner," I said. "It was wonderful."

"It was wonderful seeing you, Noel. I hope we see you again real soon." She turned to Stratton, who was watching the Alabama State Turkey Day Classic and was pretty much oblivious to us. "Honey Bun, Dylan and Noel are leaving now."

Stratton looked up. "You sure you don't want to stay and watch the game?"

"I'll be back," Dylan said. "I'm just taking Noel home."

"Case I forget, Crimson Tide rolls this Saturday at Auburn. One-thirty kickoff."

"I'll bring the dogs," Dylan said.

"You should bring Noel," he said. "That Saban's doing a heck of a job. I think we're going all the way this year." He said to me, "You're more than welcome to join us, young lady."

"Thank you. But they need me at the bookstore. We've got a really big book signing. And it's the first Saturday after Thanksgiving, so I'm thinking it will be crazy busy."

"Busier than a rented mule," he said. "It sure was nice seeing you again. Don't wait so long next time."

"That's up to your son."

"You don't need his say so to come by," he said. "Just drop by anytime."

"Thanks, Dad," Dylan said. He squatted down next to Alexis. "I'll be right back, honey. You okay?"

"No worries, Daddy," she said.

He kissed her on the forehead then we walked out of the house. After he'd pulled out into the street I said, "Alexis is at home with your parents."

"It is her home," he said. "Charlotte and Stratton are her favorite people in the world. And they think the sun rises and sets on her." He looked over. "After Susie left, my mother stepped in like a mama bear. I never even asked. It was natural. Alex spends almost every Saturday night with her. It's their cooking night. They even have matching aprons."

"That's really beautiful," I said. "I wonder what that would be like." I looked at him. "I was never close to my grandparents."

"Why is that?"

"My mother's parents weren't a part of her life. They disowned her after she married my father. My father's parents both passed away when I was still young."

"Why did they disown her?"

"I don't know. She never told me."

A few minutes later Dylan pulled up to my curb. "Home." He shut off the truck.

I breathed out slowly. "Today was nice. Thank you for inviting me."

"What a coincidence."

"What's a coincidence?"

"All these nice days I've had lately are on the same days I'm with you."

"Funny, I've noticed the same thing. Would you like to come in?"

"Absolutely."

He got out of the truck and came over and opened my door. I had already started to open it when he took it, which startled me. "Sorry, I'm not used to having my door opened for me."

"You will be if you keep hanging out with me."

We walked up to the front porch. The walkway was lightly dusted with snow, and we left imprints of our steps. I unlocked the door. We stomped the snow off our feet, then went inside. Dylan started taking off his shoes.

"You don't need to do that."

"I don't want to track snow around."

"You're right." I took my shoes off as well. "Can I get you some coffee? I have decaf."

"No, thank you."

"All right. We'll just sit." I sat down on the couch, patting the cushion next to me. "Sit."

"It sounds like you're talking to a dog."

I smiled. "Down, boy."

"Yes, ma'am." Dylan sat next to me.

"I had an author who used to talk to me like that all the time. Actually, it was Jerica Bradley—your mom's idol. She'd always finish our conversations with 'Good girl.' I'm surprised she didn't throw me a bone."

Dylan laughed. "Whatever works."

"It didn't." I leaned back against the couch. "I know you have that football game with your dad, but maybe during half-time you might want to bring Alex down to the book signing. We're having Laura Numeroff. She wrote the children's book *If You Give a Mouse a Cookie*."

"We have that book."

"I think everyone does. She's a big deal. I thought Alex might like to meet her. You wouldn't have to wait in line."

"I'll take you up on that," he said. "Alex would like that." He looked at me with a satisfied grin. "It's good having friends in high places."

I smiled back. "It will be good seeing you. Things have been so busy. I haven't been seeing enough of you."

"I feel the same. You can't get enough of a good thing," he said.

It felt good to hear that. "You think I'm a good thing?"

"Today's the best day I've had in a long time." He slightly hesitated. "I'm almost afraid to enjoy it too much."

"Why is that?"

"Because I don't want to go through losing you."

"Who says you have to lose me?"

"You haven't made up your mind about staying."

I sighed. "I know." I looked into his eyes. He looked beautiful. I said, "Do you remember the first time we kissed?"

"We were in the basement of Mark Frank's house."

"Mark Frank. I forgot about him. The only seventh grader at Hillcrest with a mustache."

"And a mullet." Dylan shook his head. "That kid pretty much lived on his own. I got in a lot of trouble at his house. Or maybe that was the problem—I didn't get in trouble. I don't think I ever saw an adult there."

"I'm surprised you remember."

"No one forgets their first kiss," he said. "It's a religious experience. Especially when it's with a girl as beautiful as you. I couldn't believe you let me kiss you. I still can't."

"A religious experience," I repeated softly.

"I've always thought there were things outside heaven worthy of worship," Dylan said. He looked into my eyes. "There are reasons to stay, Noel. I hope you'll consider that." For a moment we just looked into each other's eyes. Then he said, "Don't make me regret this."

"Regret what?"

He leaned forward and we kissed.

CHAPTER

thirty-one

If it sounds like writing, I rewrite it.

—*Elmore Leonard*

BLACK FRIDAY, NOVEMBER 27

Every Thanksgiving before my mother died followed the same pattern. After the meal was over and the dishes were done, our family would go to the bookstore to prepare for Black Friday. I asked my father why they called it Black Friday. He said, "Because that's the day American businesses get into the black." I asked what it meant to "get into the black." He replied, "It means we get to do it again next year."

My father's attention to the season was more than a nod to crass consumerism. He loved the holidays, and his store was his canvas to capture the season in all its richness. It was his aim to ensure that each of the senses were positively engaged; the sights, the sounds, the smells, and even the tastes, as we doled out plastic cups of free wassail and eggnog along with plates of Christmas-themed sugar cookies, the kind with red and green sprinkles.

His store was always crowded during these times, not just with customers but with happiness. People came from miles around to drink in the Christmas spirit and remember what it once was like to believe.

My father would schedule three or four book signings for that weekend, at least one of them with a national bestselling author. My father was the envy of local booksellers, since he had a reputation for bringing in authors that no other local bookstore could land.

The year I was eight, he brought in R. L. Stine, the author of the Goosebumps books. For about three days I was the most popular kid in school. I have no idea how my father lured one of the highest selling authors in the world to our little store in Utah, though the fact that his store reported sales to the *New York Times* bestsellers list didn't hurt.

On a side note, small city book signings aren't necessarily bad for authors. Jerica, a New Yorker, explained it best. After one up-town book signing, she said, "In Pocatello, Idaho, I'm a goddess. In New York I'm a footnote on the *What's Happening* page."

My mother and I would help run those book signings. To expedite the signing process, I would hand out Post-it Notes for people to write down the names of who they wanted their books dedicated to, while my mother would sit next to the authors, opening the books to the title page and then handing them to the author.

My mother's main job wasn't to open books but rather to engage the customer so they felt like they'd had a good experience even if the author was less than cordial. The customers always liked my mother, and more than one author was taken with her as well. She was charming, pretty, and engaging. Her death left a hole in my heart no one else could ever fill. Not even my father. Especially not my father. He had dug the hole.

This Black Friday, Wendy had scheduled two author signings. The first was a popular local radio show host named Amanda Dickson. Her self-published book was called *Behind the Mike: Twelve Years of Radio Scuttlebutt*. Ms. Dickson's local following translated into a large turnout and a lot of sales.

Our second book signing was for the *Holiday Healthy* cookbook. The signing probably would have gone well, except that the author made the mistake of giving out treats made from her recipes. They were awful. You might as well have just eaten the book.

All in all, it was another strong sales day. It was also the first Friday I hadn't received a letter from Tabula Rasa. I was admittedly disappointed. I wondered if Dylan had run out of things to say.

CHAPTER

thirty–two

If the book will be too difficult for grown-ups, then you write it for children.

—Madeleine L'Engle

SATURDAY, NOVEMBER 28

As we expected, Saturday's crowd was even larger than Friday's. Before his death, my father had gifted us one last big signing—Laura Numeroff.

Hundreds of people showed up, and the line literally stretched around the block. For more than four hours our bundled-up employees walked up and down the line handing out cups of hot wassail.

Dylan texted me when he arrived. I met him and Alexis in the back parking lot where I had saved him a space and brought them in through the employees' entrance. I escorted them past the stanchions to the front of the line.

Ms. Numeroff was personable and even got up from the table to take a picture with Alexis, something we didn't have time to let the other customers do.

That morning I had picked Ms. Numeroff up from her hotel, something my father used to do for the authors, and we'd built a quick rapport as she shared great gossip. She told me she had once dated the drummer of a famous rock band (name withheld), but he dumped her shortly after their first album took off. In her subsequent melancholy, she wrote her first *If You Give . . .* book. The series, so far, had sold more than 45 million copies, nearly triple the band's combined album sales. "Karma is sweet," she said to me.

Dylan offered to stay and help with the signing, but I sent him off to watch the football game with his father. Ms. Numeroff had a tight schedule, and we had to close the doors with people still in line so she could catch her flight out.

By the end of the day we were all exhausted. Wendy was beyond ecstatic about our success. Even though the bulk of the sales were run through credit cards, she had still emptied the cash from the register into the safe six times.

As we were locking up, she said, "Your boyfriend is cute. Was that his daughter?"

"Alexis," I said.

"She was well behaved."

"Good fathering," I said.

"We could use more of those," Wendy said.

Her comment piqued my interest. "Were you close to your father?"

"I didn't even know him. He left my mother when I was two." She turned off the front display lights, then said, "By the way, your letter came in the mail today. I left it back on the desk."

"Thank you."

"Have you figured out who's sending them?"

"I think it's Dylan."

"Maybe you should just ask him."

"If he wanted me to know, he'd tell me, right? And if it's not him, it would just be embarrassing."

"You'll figure it out."

I saved the letter for when I got home.

> *Dear Noel,*
> *Be kind. If you can't love your neighbor, be kind to them, and you may see your kindness turn to love. Do not proclaim your great love for the disadvantaged masses when you hate your next-door neighbor. The world of humanity is not the vast, unfathomable ocean, it is the lone starfish that washes up on the beach.*
>
> *Do not think of love as weakness. Love is not the fluff of greeting cards. Love is the hard, rocky shore that holds fast against the ocean's turbulent waves. Love is the soldier who lays down his life for his friends in the trenches. Love is the mother who goes to bed hungry so her children will have breakfast. Love is the opposite of self-interest, the disciples of which flee at the hint of self-sacrifice. Those without love are like the ethereal seeds of a dandelion, scattering to the wind at the first small breeze to find the next real thing.*
>
> *Tabula Rasa*

I lay the letter on the bed. "You should have been a writer, Dylan." I was glad he had come to the signing. I went to bed with him on my mind.

CHAPTER

thirty–three

Half my life is an act of revision.

—John Irving

MONDAY, NOVEMBER 30

Monday was a Monday. Our first customer of the day was a return. She was a thickset woman with thick glasses and a shrill voice. She set the book on the counter, then announced, "I need to return this book."

"Is something wrong with it?" I asked.

"Just look at it. It's not . . . *right*."

"What's not right?"

"The pages. They're cut wrong. They're uneven."

I looked at the book's edge. "Oh. You mean the deckled edge. It's a decorative feature."

"Decorative?"

"Yes, the publisher had the pages trimmed like that on

purpose. It gives it the appearance of an old-fashioned hand-crafted book."

"Why would a publisher purposely ruin a book?"

"Like I said, it's decorative. People like it. It's antiquarian."

"Well, I'm not into astrology. I just want the book with normal, smooth edges."

"I'm sorry, but the publisher doesn't make it that way."

"Then I'd like a discount for a damaged book."

The rest of the day seemed to follow the same flow. I was glad when Grace came in, but even she seemed a little quiet. The book she bought was below her usual standards. "It's not for me," she said, as if embarrassed to be seen with the book. "It's a gift."

As I rang her up, she abruptly asked, "When did your relationship with your father sour?"

"How did you know it soured?"

"Your father and I were close," she reminded me.

"I suppose when I was old enough to know the truth."

"What truth?"

"That my father wasn't who I thought he was."

She let my words sit for a moment, then replied, "I think that's still true."

"Why do you ask?"

"I don't know. Curious, perhaps." She took her book and walked out of the store.

CHAPTER

thirty–four

The Agee woman told us for three quarters of an hour how she came to write her beastly book, when a simple apology was all that was required.

—P. G. Wodehouse

TUESDAY, DECEMBER 1

I t was a little before ten o'clock and I'd just finished ringing up a customer when my phone rang. I looked down to check the number. It was a New York area code.

"Hello."

"Noel. It's Natasha. I hope I didn't wake you."

I don't know what surprised me more, hearing her voice or her voice's pleasant lilt.

"No, I'm at work."

"You've already got a job?"

"I've got a bookstore. And yes, I got my things, if that's why you're calling."

"Not why I called," she said. "It turns out that I shouldn't have been so efficient in cleaning your office. I have good news. I'm calling to offer you your job back."

Now this really wasn't making sense. "You're rehiring me?"

"You know, I never felt good about letting you go. So I talked to HR, and saner heads prevailed. If you're amenable to coming back, we'll just keep your arrangement as is and consider your absence paid leave."

Now we were entering the Twilight Zone. "What about my authors?"

"There will probably be a few changes, but we'll sort that out once you're back. When will you be back in New York?"

"I don't know," I said. My mind was still reeling. "Why are you really calling?"

Natasha hesitated. "It's just what I said. I called to offer you your job back."

"Five weeks ago you tossed me like a bad query letter. I know this world. Everything happens for a reason, and I'm pretty sure it wasn't because you missed me. So what really happened?"

Natasha groaned. "I always said you were smart. I'm sure you'll eventually find out, so here's the deal. Ms. Bradley didn't like the editor we gave her. In fact, she didn't want to work with any editor but you. She informed us that she would either work with you at our imprint or find another publishing house to hire you and she'd publish with them."

"Jerica said that?"

"Word for word. And you know Jerica. It's her way or the highway."

I shook my head. "So the Tin Woman has a heart."

"I wouldn't go that far," Natasha said. "So, when can we expect you back?"

"I'm not sure I'm coming back."

"What do you mean?"

"I'm thinking of staying in Utah."

Long pause. "You can't be serious."

"I need to think this over. But considering the circumstance, I'd say a raise is a good place to start."

"I can make that happen."

"All right, I'll let you know."

"You let me know," she repeated. "The sooner the better. Jerica wants an answer yesterday."

"Like I said, I'll let you know."

"Thank you," Natasha said. "And Noel, Jerica aside, I'm glad you're coming back. You really are a good editor."

"Thank you." I hung up the phone. *Never saw that coming.*

Dear Noel,
There are real dangers in this life, far too many to enumerate. Fortunately for all of us, we were blessed with the gift of fear. Fear acknowledged is a gift. It sharpens our senses, heightens our awareness, and strengthens our muscles. It is the warning bell before the crash.

Fear-mindedness is a curse. The greatest shackles in our lives have always been those forged by our own fears.

Courage is not the opposite of fear, as courage cannot exist without it. Courage is the decision to proceed in spite of fear. You have shown great courage in your life. But sometimes the things we fear most are not demons, but angels. Know the difference. Do not fear to love because of the chance of loss. This life consists of loss. It must be. We can bemoan what we have lost, or we can be grateful to have been blessed with something to mourn. The choice is yours. To avoid love because of the possibility of losing it is like poisoning ourselves to avoid being murdered.

Tabula Rasa

CHAPTER

thirty-five

Good prose is like a windowpane.

—*George Orwell*

THURSDAY, DECEMBER 3

D ylan had two employees out with the flu, leaving him working extra shifts. I missed him, but, as he said, "I'm lucky to be miserably overworked."

I was surprised when I got a call from him Thursday night after work.

"What are you doing?"

"Trying to decide what to eat for dinner," I said.

"Want to go ice skating?"

"Tonight?"

"Yes."

"Just us?"

"And Alex."

"That's spontaneous."

"I was feeling spontaneous. And I was missing you."

"When?"

"I was thinking of leaving in ten minutes."

"Have you had dinner?"

"Just mac and cheese. I told Alex we'd get a treat after."

"I'll be ready."

"Then we'll be right over. Dress warm."

"Darn, I was going to wear a bikini."

"Don't let me dissuade you."

"Bye."

I made myself some coffee and English crumpets, which I spread with butter and some homemade apricot jam I found in one of the cupboards. Dylan pulled up about twenty minutes later. Before he could get out, I ran out to his truck and hopped in. I leaned over and we kissed.

"Hi, Miss Noel," Alexis said. She was buckled in the back seat.

"Hi, Alex."

"We're going ice-skating."

"I know. Have you been skating before?"

"Yes. I take classes. I'm pretty good."

"I'm not." I turned to Dylan. "What prompted this little outing?"

"I told you, Alex and I were missing you." He turned to me. "Mostly me."

I kissed him on the cheek. "I was missing you too."

We drove downtown to the Gallivan Center. The Gallivan ice-skating rink was outdoors and seasonal, opening shortly before Thanksgiving and staying open until February. It reminded me a little of the Rockefeller Center ice rink, sans the gilded statue of Prometheus and the massive Christmas tree. That's not to say it wasn't decorated for the season. The rink was surrounded by a small forest of bedecked evergreen trees with more than a quarter million Christmas lights.

When we arrived the rink was surrounded by displaced skaters while the Zamboni resurfaced the ice, but by the time we had rented and donned our skates, the rink was open again. The ice was flooded by a changing array of colors from spotlights hanging above it.

Dylan and I were at about the same skating skill level—somewhere between dangerous and embarrassing—and we clumsily skated counterclockwise around the perimeter of the rink with Alex between us, each of us holding one of her mittened hands.

We didn't last long. It was a cold night, the temperature falling into the upper twenties. We skated for less than an hour, then turned in our skates.

"I have a surprise," Dylan said as we walked to his truck.

"Yes?"

"You'll see." We drove up the Avenues and pulled into the parking lot of a small brown-bricked building near the hospital.

"Have you ever been here?" he asked, turning off his truck.

"I have no idea where 'here' is," I said.

"Hatch Family Chocolates. About six years ago they had a TV series on TLC. It was called *Little Chocolatiers*."

"Wait, they're little people. Did I say that right?"

Dylan nodded. "Steve and Kate."

"I watched a few episodes of that. How did I not know that was in Utah?"

The chocolate shop had at least a dozen tables inside, and almost all of them were taken, crowded with families and groups of young people. A line wrapped around the long glass display cases of handmade chocolates, truffles, caramels, fudge, and ice cream.

"Dad, can I have an ice cream cone?"

"Do you want a cone or a hot chocolate?" Dylan asked.

"Yes."

Dylan laughed. "All right, for Christmas's sake."

Dylan ordered three cups of their famous hot cocoa with melted bars of milk chocolate. He also bought me a small box of chocolate mint truffles to take home.

"You know the way to a woman's heart," I said.

"At least yours," he said. "I hope."

As we walked back to the truck Alexis looked up at me. "Noel?"

"Yes, honey?"

"Will you be my mommy?"

The question hung in the frozen air. Dylan said, "Alex, Noel's our good friend."

All I could think to say was "Thank you for asking."

I thought about her question all the way home. I wondered if Dylan was doing the same, because neither of us talked as Alex fell asleep in the back seat. We stopped at my house, and Dylan walked me to the door. "I'm sorry about that," he said.

"It's okay. She doesn't have a mother. I understand."

He looked at me gratefully. "Thank you for understanding."

"Thank you for tonight." I lifted my bag of truffles. "And the chocolates. I'm glad you called. You thwarted yet another lonely night."

"Maybe I can thwart another one," he said. "One of my clients works for Ballet West. He offered me tickets to the *Nutcracker* a week from Sunday."

"I haven't been to the *Nutcracker* since I danced in it."

"You danced in it?"

"Just one year. I was a mouse. I'd love to go."

"Splendid. The show starts at seven, so why don't I pick you up at five and we'll have dinner at my parents'. Charlotte's cooking."

"I'm not going to pass that up. Thank you."

He leaned forward and we kissed. It felt so good. He felt good. "Things are too busy these days," he said. "For both of us. It will be better after the season when things slow down. Right? As long as you don't go anywhere."

I didn't know what to say. I still hadn't told him about Natasha's call. "You're right. Everything will be better."

CHAPTER

thirty—six

FRIDAY, DECEMBER 4

Dear Noel,
As you sail your way through the sea of humanity,
you will discover that most people don't want truth.
They want confirmation. Truth has always been
frightening to those clinging to shaky ladders of belief.
The more indefensible the belief, the tighter their grip.
Let them be. Truth does not require confirmation nor
consensus to endure. Truth is patient. It can afford to
be. In the end it will have its way.

To walk in truth is to have the humility to listen
to what you don't want to hear and say what others
don't want to know. Humility is the power to admit
that you may be wrong.

Admitting to false beliefs is not weakness, it is the
first step on the path to truth. And make no mistake,
there is no such thing as individual truth, only individual
perception. Perception is subjective, but truth isn't. Hold
your hand over a candle and you'll understand.

Tabula Rasa

CHAPTER

thirty—seven

Don't edit your own soul according to the fashion.
Rather, follow your most intense obsessions mercilessly.

—Anne Rice

MONDAY, DECEMBER 7

Monday afternoon Grace came in at her usual time. She dropped her chosen book on the counter—a massive nine-hundred-page tome—then handed me her credit card. I scanned the book.

"I have news," I said.

She smiled. "Good news, I hope."

"I'm not sure." I glanced around. "I haven't told anyone yet, but my publisher offered me my job back."

She looked pleased. "That is definitely good news. So they finally realized they can't live without you?"

"It's a little more complicated than that. They only did it because one of my big authors, Jerica Bradley, said she'd only work with me."

"That *is* a little more complicated," she said. She looked into my face. "Is that what you want? To be an editor for the rest of your life?"

"It's what I went to school for."

"That's not what I asked."

I was still getting used to Grace's directness. "I don't know."

"Let me ask you this. If you knew that whatever you did you would be a great success at it, what would you do?"

"I'd be a writer."

"There you have it. You have the connections to agents and publishing houses, and your father put you in a situation where you could have the time to write."

I handed back her credit card. "My father wanted to be a writer."

"Your father *was* a writer," she said. "He completed two novels, had two more in progress, and wrote a children's book. They were all exceptional. Have you read any of them?"

"I only knew of one. And I never read it."

"Pity," she said. "I think you would have taken it to your publisher if you had. They're among the few I have kept." She lifted the book she'd just purchased. "Unlike this one. I have a feeling that"—she looked at the cover—"*City on Fire* might end up on fire, if you know what I mean."

"Then why are you buying it?"

"The *New York Times* called the author's talent as thick as the book, *USA Today* called it epic, and the *New York Post* called it, and I quote, 'a steaming pile of literary dung.' I love books with mixed reviews. I thought I'd give the author a chance." She winked. "Who knows? Every now and then an author will surprise you." She put the book into her tote. "Good luck with your decision." She turned and walked out of the store.

CHAPTER

thirty-eight

You should write because you love the shape of stories.

—Annie Proulx

TUESDAY, DECEMBER 8

I t had been a month, a week, and a day since I started at the bookstore. It had been rough at first, but there had been steady progress made in my and Wendy's relationship.

I destroyed it all in just five minutes.

"I'm thinking of changing the bookstore's name," I said as Wendy and I sorted through some returns.

Wendy looked at me as if I'd just blasphemed. "To what?"

"It Was a Dark and Stormy Bookstore."

Like everyone else, she looked at me blankly.

"It's a reference to—"

"I know what it's a reference to," she said. "It's the opening line of Edward Bulwer-Lytton's 1830 novel *Paul Clifford*, though today most people know it from Snoopy typing on top of his doghouse."

"Then you don't approve . . . ?"

"As your father used to say, 'Don't fix what ain't broken.'" She stood to go, then added, "By the way, Lytton also created a few other notable phrases, such as 'The pen is mightier than the sword' and 'The almighty dollar.' In case you're obsessed with the man." She walked away.

"Not as obsessed as you are with my father," I said to myself.

She didn't speak to me the rest of the day. That afternoon she left my letter on the front counter.

> *Dear Noel,*
> *Be grateful. To live each day in gratitude is to live in power. Gratitude is the opposite of despair. Gratitude is power and the root of all happiness. It is the power to find happiness. Show me ingratitude and I will show you misery. Like love, gratitude is also a choice. There are none so impoverished as those who don't acknowledge the abundance of their lives.*
>
> *Tabula Rasa*

CHAPTER

thirty–nine

FRIDAY, DECEMBER 11

Dear Noel,
Love. Love is the single greatest choice you can make
in your life. Make no mistake: Love is a choice. It
is not something that happens to you nor a hole
you fall into. It is not an accident. Those things are
mere counterfeits of love, capricious hormones that
come and go like pigeons after breadcrumbs. Love
is a choice, a decision, that is grown and cultivated,
pruned at times and patiently cared for. If properly
nourished, it will someday grow into something too
big to uproot—something that will provide shade
and sustenance, constantly climbing upward and
spreading its shelter over others.

If you believe you must earn love, as many do, or
require it of others, you do not understand its nature.
Love earned ceases to be love. It is wage. Love.

Tabula Rasa

CHAPTER

forty

No tears in the writer, no tears in the reader.

—*Robert Frost*

SUNDAY, DECEMBER 13

I t had been more than a decade since I'd been to the ballet. I had brought only one nice dress from New York, the one I had worn for my father's funeral. I spent extra time getting ready. I had nothing but time, and I wanted to look nice. Not just because it was the ballet but for Dylan.

Dylan picked me up a few minutes before five. My first thought was how handsome he looked in his tailored suit.

"Where's Alex?"

"She's already at my parents'." He looked at me with a sort of awe in his eyes. "You look stunning, Noel. You always look beautiful, but . . ."

I smiled. "I clean up well. You look nice too."

"Thank you." He put out his arm. "Shall we go?"

A few minutes later we parked in Dylan's parents' driveway and went inside. Alexis ran to us as we walked in. Actually, she ran to me. "Noel!"

She was wearing a pretty little hunter-green velvet dress with pearl buttons, and her hair was pulled back in a bun like a ballerina's.

"You look very pretty," I said.

"Thank you."

"Did Grandma do your hair?"

"No, Daddy did."

"Really?" I looked at Dylan. "That's impressive."

"It's no big deal," he said. "I was good at tying knots in the Boy Scouts."

I laughed.

"Actually, I just got tired of driving her to Grandma's all the time."

Charlotte already had dinner on the table. "I hope y'all weren't expecting anything too fancy," she said. "Just chicken and dumplings. Strat calls it comfort food."

"Sounds perfect," I said. "We all need more comfort."

"Amen to that," Charlotte said.

As usual, the main course was one part of a much larger meal. There was grilled corn, steamed vegetables, and cornbread. It wasn't just the food that was comforting. So was being with Dylan's family. It was the only place in my world back then that resembled a home.

After we finished eating, I offered to help clean up, but Charlotte wouldn't hear of it.

"No, dear. You have the ballet to get to. You don't want to

be late. It's not like the movies. They don't let you just walk in at your leisure."

The Capitol Theatre on Second South is one of Salt Lake's oldest buildings. It was built in 1913 as a vaudeville house called the Orpheum until fourteen years later when its name was changed.

During the holidays the *Nutcracker* was performed at the theatre three times a day, and we entered the lobby against a stream of people leaving the building. It had been more than twenty-three years since I had been there, and the theater, like me, had undergone an extensive renovation, inside and out.

We surrendered our tickets at the door, then went into the hall to find our seats. The theater was ornately designed in the classic style of the Italian Renaissance, like many of the opera and ballet houses of Old Europe. The seats were red velvet with polished dark wood arms, stark against the ivory-colored walls with chalk-white panels and gold-leaf accents.

The stage bulged slightly with the orchestra pit, settled at the base of a massive red curtain with a thick gold-fringed hem. I remember, as a young girl, being on the other side of that curtain, waiting with the other little girls for our chance to dance.

As the conductor walked out to applause, a long-dormant excitement rose in my stomach, which grew as the iconic chords of Tchaikovsky resonated throughout the theater. I had watched the performance more than fifty times, though always from behind, and it was peculiar seeing the production as it was designed to be seen. The way my parents saw it. The way they saw me.

I was transfixed by it all, as memories flooded into my heart. As a girl, my love of dancing had been everything and I gave it up back when I had given up everything else I once loved.

As the performance progressed, my feeling of excitement changed to a heaviness in my stomach and chest, almost in contrast to the ethereal weightlessness of the dancers floating across the stage. In a sense, ballet is a lie—an illusion. It is made to look effortless but requires incredible physical stamina, strength, and pain. I have seen blood drip from ballerinas' feet as they removed their toe shoes.

My life was also a lie. In this sense, I had never stopped trying to make things look easy and right.

The final scene of Act 1 was the battle scene between the soldiers and the mice—the scene I had danced in. Watching the girls prance across the stage in their little mouse costumes brought a flood of emotion. I looked over at Dylan, who was smiling, intent on the performance. Alexis was curled up against him, her hand on his arm, her head against his chest. There was something inexplicably powerful about what I was experiencing, both on stage and in the seat next to me— something I had buried deep within my psyche. I suddenly had a flashback of my father carrying me out of this very theater, my head against his chest, the smell of his cologne in my nostrils.

As I looked at them, tears began falling down my cheeks.

A few at first, then in greater numbers. My chest constricted. I was suddenly having trouble breathing and felt nauseous. Dylan glanced over at me, his concern evident in his eyes. "Are you okay?" he whispered.

"No." I stood and hurried out of the performance, in too much pain to be embarrassed by the disapproving glances I got as I ran up the aisle toward the exit.

CHAPTER

forty-one

If you really want to know yourself, start by writing a book.

—Shereen El Feki

Dylan came out after me, carrying Alexis. I was grateful that he didn't ask what was wrong. I couldn't have explained it if he did. All he said was, "I'll take you home."

The drive home was silent. It seemed that lately all our drives home were silent.

As usual, Dylan walked me to the doorstep. He never came inside when Alexis was with us, and right now I wished she wasn't with us. I wanted him to come inside. I desperately wanted him to hold me and never let me go. But there was something else inside me that was pushing back—a force growing louder and stronger, shouting at me to run before it was too late; screaming that love was an illusion. There were no true relationships. No one stayed together anymore. Not my mother and father. Not my husband. And not Dylan. No one.

"I'm sorry we had to leave early," I said. "I hope Alex is okay."

"She's fine," he said gently. "Were there too many memories?"

"Ghosts of Christmas Past," I said. "Just too many ghosts." I closed my eyes. "It's hard being back."

"I know." He put his arms around me. "Are you feeling okay? You look a little pale."

"I just need some sleep. I'll be better tomorrow."

"Then I'll let you get some sleep." He kissed me, then stepped back, still holding my hand. "I'll call you tomorrow. Get some rest."

He walked off to his truck. I stood on the porch watching as he drove away. Then I walked inside and shut the door and leaned against it. I suddenly felt dizzy.

The attack started with ringing in my ears growing louder and louder until I collapsed to the floor and the ringing became screaming—my mother screaming at my father to get off her. Then it was me being held down. My father was on top of me, holding me as I struggled, powerless against him. My clothes were drenched in sweat. Only now it wasn't my mother screaming, it was me. That's when I passed out.

CHAPTER

forty-two

How vain it is to sit down to write when you have not stood up to live.

—Henry David Thoreau

MONDAY, DECEMBER 14

Sometime in the night I had gotten to my room and into bed. I woke with a headache, but my heart hurt more. It pounded in panic. I had to leave. It didn't matter where I went. I wasn't running to something, I was running away from this, whatever this was. I couldn't think of any other way to escape than to fasten myself to something that would take me with it—like tying an anchor to my leg and throwing it into the sea. There was only one thing like that in my life. I picked up the phone and dialed Natasha.

"Noel," she said. "Good morning."

"I'm sorry I took so long to get back to you."

"I figured you probably had some legal things to work out with your father's death. So are you coming back to us?"

"Yes," I said, fixing myself to the word.

"Wonderful. How soon can you be here?"

"It might take a while. I don't have a place to live."

"We can help with that. We have a corporate contract with the Hilton. We'll put you up for a week or two while you find a place."

"That's very generous of you."

"We just want you back," she said. "And you made the right choice."

"Thank you for taking me back."

I hung up. I didn't know if it was the right choice. But it felt like my only one.

I felt numb as I drove to work. The store was busy all day, and I didn't stop for lunch. I couldn't have eaten anyway, as my stomach ached. As usual, I was at the front counter when Grace came in. She picked out her book, then brought it over to me. "Here we are."

I couldn't get the scanner to read the book, so I typed in the ISBN. I could feel the weight of her gaze on me.

"How are you, Noel?"

"I took the job," I blurted out. It sounded like a murder confession at a police interrogation.

She looked at me silently, then asked, "The editor job in New York?"

"Yes." I expected that she would be disappointed in me after I had told her that being an editor wasn't really my dream. Or maybe I was just projecting my own disappointment in myself onto her.

"Then you'll be leaving us soon."

"Right after Christmas." I handed her the book, and she put it in her tote and then looked back at me. As I looked into her eyes I sensed no judgment or condemnation. Just kindness. She reached out and gently touched my hand. "They're fortunate to have you. But their gain is our loss. You will be missed."

CHAPTER

forty–three

A writer is someone for whom writing is more difficult
than it is for other people.

—Thomas Mann

Around three in the afternoon I got a call from my father's attorney. I hadn't heard from him since he'd come by the house my first week back.

"Noel, it's Christopher Smalls. I just wanted to let you know that I have a check from the insurance company. I can mail it to you or you're welcome to come get it. I would bring it by, but I have appointments."

"Thank you; I can come get it. Where are you?"

"My office is in the Avenues. I'll text you the address."

I told Wendy that I had to leave early. I don't think she was happy, but, frankly, she hadn't been happy with me ever since I told her I wanted to change the store's name.

A half hour later I was driving up a one-way street to the attorney's office. It was an old slate-bricked home with a large plate-glass window emblazoned in gold with the name of several other professionals, including a CPA and a marriage counselor.

Mr. Smalls greeted me in the lobby as I walked in, then led me to his office and shut the door behind us. His wood furniture was scuffed and outdated, as if it had been purchased at an estate sale.

"Have a seat," he said.

I sat down. "I only have a few minutes. I'd like to get to the bank before it closes."

"This won't take long." He handed me an envelope. I pulled back the flap and took out the check. It was a yellow safety-paper check made out to me for a million dollars.

"Ever seen a check for a million dollars?" he asked.

"Not with my name on it. That's a lot of zeroes."

"More than I'll ever see." He smiled. "Still planning on getting out of Dodge?"

I put the check in my purse. "I'm going back to New York. So I guess I'll be selling the house. Do you know a good real estate agent?"

"We have one here in this office. Shelley specializes in residential real estate. I can introduce you to her right now, or I can snag her business card for you."

"Her card is fine for now. Like I said, I'd like to get to the bank." I stood. "Also, do you know how I would go about selling the bookstore?"

"That's a bit more complicated. But I'd be happy to look into that for you as well."

"I'd appreciate it." I shook his hand. "Thank you, Mr. Smalls."

"Your very welcome. Good luck."

I walked out of the office carrying a million-dollar check, feeling like people would stare if they knew.

I banked with a large national institution that had a branch near my home in Sugar House. I filled out a deposit slip, then walked up to an open window and handed it, along with the check, to the teller. What happened next was a little surreal. The young man asked for my ID, then suddenly froze when he saw the amount on the check. He furtively glanced up at me and said, "Just a minute." He carried the check over to someone in a small office. That person looked at the check and then over at me, then stood and walked through a door at the back of the bank. A few minutes later a handsome, fortysomething man in an Armani suit walked up behind me.

"Excuse me, Ms. Book?"

I turned around. "Yes?"

He put out his hand. "My name is Roland Cox. Thank you for your business. You're in the wrong side of the bank."

The letter I got the next day seemed especially appropriate. And, in a way, prophetic. I wondered if Dylan had sensed that something critical was happening in my life.

> *Dear Noel,*
> *Life is difficult. The sooner we accept this, the*
> *sooner we can get on living it. Be grateful for your*
> *challenges. Without great mountains we cannot*

reach great heights and we were born to reach great heights. Never give up on your dreams. Too many in this world stop at speed bumps mistaking them for walls. Most obstacles are just stepping-stones on the path to success and failure is merely a temporary space on the gameboard of life waiting for the next roll of the dice.

Tabula Rasa

How was I going to tell him that I was leaving?

CHAPTER

forty–four

There's no such thing as perfect writing,
just like there's no such thing as perfect despair.

—*Haruki Murakami*

THURSDAY, DECEMBER 17

O n Thursday afternoon I let Wendy know I would be taking a longer than usual lunch break. For the first time, I drove to Dylan's suit shop.

Dylan's was located less than ten minutes from the bookstore in a strip mall on the slope of the Wasatch mountains. The mall was decorated with strings of Christmas lights and giant foil snowflakes hanging from the parking lot light fixtures.

The upper parking lot was full, and I ended up parking below ground and walking up to Dylan's store. A large sign above the door read

Dylan's
Quality Men's Suits and Apparel

In the display window were glossy black mannequins dressed in black or navy suits with crisp white shirts with French cuffs and bright silk ties with matching pocket squares. Blue foil snowflakes hung from fishing line around them.

As I opened the door, an electronic bell rang. Dylan was standing near the back at a cash register helping a customer. He looked up at me with a surprised expression. "Noel."

I waved. "Hi."

The older gentleman he was helping turned around to see who he was talking to.

"I'll be right with you," Dylan said, sounding unusually professional.

A younger, dark-featured man in a suit and open collar walked up to me from the adjacent showroom. "May I help you?"

"I'm here to see Dylan."

He turned to Dylan. "Boss, can I finish up for you?"

"Bennett and I are just about done." Dylan said to his client, "This beautiful woman is my friend, Noel. She was my very first girlfriend back in seventh grade."

"Pleased to meet you, Noel," he said. Then, to Dylan, "Tell me, how did an ugly guy like you land such a beauty?"

"Money," Dylan said dryly. "She's a gold digger."

"I'm standing right here," I said.

Dylan handed the man back a credit card, then the vinyl suit bag hanging from a post extending from the counter. "There you go, Bennett. Have fun on your cruise. Don't fall overboard, and come back with the same woman you go with."

The man laughed. "I'll do my best." He slung the bag over his shoulder, then said to me as he walked past, "Take the scoundrel for everything he's worth." He walked out of the store.

Dylan walked out from around the counter and we kissed. "What are you doing here?"

"I was in the area, so I came to see where you work."

"Why were you in the area?"

I grinned. "To see where you work."

He put his hands in his pockets. "So, this is it, Chez Dylan. What do you think?"

I looked around the store. The space was tastefully designed with a modern, yet elegant motif. The walls were lined with high-gloss burl walnut cabinetry, and the floor was an onyx-like tile that reflected the overhead rows of track lighting.

"It's very chic," I said.

"Don't sound too surprised."

"You can't blame me," I said. "In school your entire wardrobe consisted of Pink Floyd T-shirts and army fatigues."

"That was the old me. I had this inner clotheshorse fighting to get out."

"Looks like it succeeded. I have good news. My check

from the insurance company came. I'm officially a million-aire."

"Wow. How does that feel?"

"I don't think it's sunk in yet."

"I guess that makes me the gold digger."

"Well, gold digger, I was hoping you had time for lunch."

"I'll make time." He turned to the other man. "Adesh, I'm going out for an hour. You okay?"

"I'm good, boss."

"And totally disregard what she just said about being a millionaire."

He looked at me. "You're a millionaire?"

"I told you to disregard that," Dylan said. He turned back to me. "Where would you like to go for lunch? Zurich?"

"I knew I shouldn't have told you," I said. "What restaurants do you have around here?"

"There's an Irish pub just across the lot."

"Is it good?"

"Do you like bangers and mash? Guinness pie?"

"I don't think so."

"Then you won't like it. How about ramen or sushi?"

"I like them both."

"There's a Japanese restaurant up the road. I'll drive."

Dylan took me to a small restaurant called Kobe. We sat ourselves at a table for two.

"This place is famous for its ramen," Dylan said. "But the sushi is good too."

"I don't know if I trust inland sushi."

"Now you're just sounding jaded," he said. "The owner here is from Japan. He studied under Eiji Ichimura, one of the greatest sushi chefs in the world."

"Never heard of him," I said.

"Have you ever heard of the restaurant Ichimura in New York?"

"On the Upper East Side? Everyone has."

"That's his sushi bar."

"My apologies to the chef."

We both ordered ramen. After our waitress left, Dylan said, "So aside from your millions, how's your bookstore doing?"

"I have *a* million, not millions. And it seems to be doing well. I didn't realize how busy it was. I guess I kind of fantasized that my father sat around all day drinking coffee and cursing Amazon."

"Your bookstore doesn't have coffee."

"In my fantasy it did."

A few minutes later our waitress brought out our meals. I had ordered the Tonkotsu with pork belly ramen, topped with mushrooms and a soft-boiled egg. Dylan had ordered the Kimchi ramen. For a moment we ate in silence. Then Dylan said, "A million dollars. You know, if you invest smart, you'll never have to work again."

"Then what would I do?"

"You'll write your book. That's what you've always wanted."

After I didn't say anything he said, "I'm not saying you won't work, I'm just saying you don't have to." His mouth rose in a large smile. "The best part is, now there's no reason for you to go back to New York."

The words struck me like a hammer. I looked down for a moment, then said, "Dylan, I have to tell you something."

My tone must have betrayed the gravity of what I had to share, as his smile fled.

"What is it?"

I took a deep breath. "When I came back to Utah, I only planned to be here a few days. A few weeks at the most. It's been almost two months." I looked into his eyes. "Dylan, this was never part of the plan."

"What wasn't?"

"Us."

He looked stunned. "Are you ending us?"

"I should have told you sooner. They've offered me my job back."

"The publishing house?"

I nodded.

"And you're going to take it?"

"I fly back the day after Christmas." The silence was awkward. Finally I said, "What do I have here?"

I regretted the words as they came out of my mouth.

"Apparently nothing," he replied softly, his eyes showing his pain.

"I'm sorry, I didn't mean that."

"There's another meaning?" He took a deep breath, then said, "We should go."

"You haven't eaten," I said.

"I need to go," he said.

"All right."

Dylan paid the bill and we drove back to his store in

silence. As we pulled into the mall he asked, "Where are you parked?"

"I'm in the lower garage. But you can drop me off here."

"I'll take you to your car." He drove down the parking ramp. I pointed out my car and he pulled up behind it. For a moment we just sat there. The pain was palpable. Finally I said, "It's not like I'll never be back."

"No you won't." He looked into my eyes. "It's like you said, there's nothing here." To my surprise, there were tears in his eyes. He reached up and wiped away a tear. "Look at that. The second time as well."

I didn't say anything. I didn't know what to say. He leaned forward and kissed me on the cheek. "Good luck, Noel. I hope you find what you're looking for."

I got out of the truck and he drove away. I got into my car and cried.

CHAPTER

forty–five

I love deadlines, I like the whooshing sound they make as they fly by.

—Douglas Adams

FRIDAY, DECEMBER 18

It was only a week before Christmas. Eight days before I returned to New York. My heart ached. I couldn't believe how much I missed Dylan.

As long as I was burning bridges, I had one more to bring down. That afternoon I took Wendy aside. "We need to talk," I said. "In private."

"All right." We went into the office. Wendy locked the door, then sat on top of her desk. "What's up?"

"I'm going back to New York."

She sat quietly for a moment, then said, "I thought you might." The next question hung in the air between us. "What are you doing with the bookstore?"

"I'm going to sell it."

Something, pain or anger, flashed in her eyes. She took a deep breath. "When?"

"I'll put it up after the New Year."

Her eyes welled up. "When do you leave for New York?"

"The twenty-sixth."

Neither of us spoke for a moment. Then I said, "I'm sure whoever buys it will want you to stay."

She took a tissue from her desk and wiped her eyes. "We'll see."

The silence grew awkward. Finally, I said, "I'm sorry."

She stood. "I've got work to do."

The rest of the day was miserable. Several times I caught Wendy crying. Cyndee asked me what was wrong. I told her I didn't know. For the first time since I'd worked with Wendy, she left early. Maybe for the first time ever. She didn't say goodbye.

> *Dear Noel,*
> *Too many live their lives as if they'll live on this*
> *Earth forever, scheming and building sand empires*
> *that will fall at the next wave of time. Ultimately, the*
> *only empire worth building is one of the soul, as the*
> *heart alone exists outside of time and physics. We*
> *all arrived on Earth with a round-trip ticket. We*
> *are sojourners and star travelers, all of us—campers*
> *from the Great Beyond. While it behooves us to*
> *leave the campground better than we found it, we*
> *are fools to put down stakes or pour foundations on*
> *unclaimable ground. One does not build a cathedral*
> *for Easter Sunday.*
>
> *Tabula Rasa*

CHAPTER

forty–six

Get it down. Take chances. It may be bad,
but it's the only way you can do anything good.

—William Faulkner

SATURDAY–SUNDAY, DECEMBER 19–20

According to the marketing gurus and their charts, the Saturday before Christmas is the busiest shopping day of the year. They call it Super Saturday. It was anything but that. Business was good, the customers plentiful, but the day was miserable. To my surprise, Wendy didn't act angry or bitter, as I'd expected. She just seemed sad—like she was grieving again. I think she was. She had grieved my father. Now she was grieving the death of the store.

I counted the minutes until we closed and I could go home and suffer alone.

That night I had a dream about Dylan. It wasn't a bad dream. In fact, it was sweet. He was loving me. When I woke, I wished it had been a bad dream. I could have dealt better with that. I wouldn't be left craving him.

I had assumed I wouldn't see Dylan again. Maybe ever. But I was wrong. Sunday evening I was on the Internet looking through a listing of apartments in Brooklyn when the doorbell rang. I looked out through the peephole. Dylan was standing there in his leather bomber jacket. His hands were behind his back.

I opened the door.

"Hi," he said.

"What do you want?" I asked, sounding harsher than I intended.

"Now there's an irrelevant question." He brought a box out from behind his back. "I bought you a Christmas-birthday present." He offered me the gift. "What did you call it, a 'two-in-one'?"

"I can't take it."

"You mean *won't*."

I just looked at him.

"Look, this isn't some pathetic attempt at getting you back. I had already bought it, so I figured I might as well give it to you."

I still just stood there.

"C'mon, Noel. It's just a birthday present."

I exhaled slowly. "All right." I took it from him. "Thank you."

"You can open it."

I furtively glanced up at him, then looked back down at the gift. I tore the paper back, revealing a heavy black hinged box. I lifted its lid to expose a beautiful black resin Montblanc pen with a gold nib.

"It's for writing your book. When you're ready."

I looked up at him. "Thank you. That was very thoughtful."

"I'm a thoughtful guy."

Emotion rose in my chest. "I'm sorry."

Dylan raised his hand. "We've already done this." He looked at me for a moment then said, "But there is something that still needs to be said. May I?"

I nodded.

"I've spent most of my life dealing with abandonment. It's a real thing, you know, not just some trending psychobabble. When you're a kid and your parents give you away, it does something to your wiring.

"But, over time, I've learned some things about it. Things that help. Humans are born vulnerable. If they don't have care, they die. So, the fear of abandonment is hardwired into us for survival. We fear abandonment even as we fear death. It's that primal.

"The thing is, when you're a kid, there's no way to make sense of that. My parents gave me away like I was a stick of gum. I'm an adult and I still can't make sense of that. Part of me wants to hunt them down and make them explain.

"But the truth is, my inner self doesn't blame them. It blames me. It's in there asking, *What's wrong with me that they didn't love me?* We wonder why we're so unlovable.

"Noel, we're no different. Your mother left. Your father sent you away. Your husband left. How do you process that? How can you just say, *It's them, not me,* and believe it?"

His voice cracked. "Sometimes it feels like the only way to deal with that fear is to push people away. Because the chance that you might really be unlovable is much too terrifying to face.

"It's a pretty simple conclusion. In fact, I figured that out when I was Alex's age—that the only way I was going to make it through life was by going it alone. That's why I burned through foster homes like a wildfire. I punished anyone who took a chance on me. And I had to prove to myself that I didn't need them. That I didn't need anyone.

"And then Stratton and Charlotte came along. I tried to push them away, but the harder I pushed, the tighter they held. They did the impossible. They convinced me I was lovable. So when Susan abandoned me. I still believed I was okay. And my reward is that I have this beautiful little girl whose life centers around me.

"I'm telling you this, Noel, because the only difference between us is that someone got through to me. I want you to know that you are lovable. And no one can prove otherwise. Not even you."

We both stood there in silence. Then he said, "Okay, that's my speech. I'll let you go. I love you. I think I always have. And I probably always will."

Tears were streaming down my face. I wanted to be loved by him more than I could say. But he was right. The terror was just too great.

He kissed my cheek, and then as he stepped off the porch I said, "Dylan. Thank you for the letters."

He looked at me with a quizzical expression. "What letters?"

"The ones you've been sending me."

He shook his head. "Must be some other fool." Then he walked to his truck and drove away.

CHAPTER

forty–seven

Here is a lesson in creative writing.
First rule: Do not use semicolons. They are transvestite
hermaphrodites representing absolutely nothing.
All they do is show you've been to college.

—Kurt Vonnegut

MONDAY, DECEMBER 21

Four days until Christmas; five more days until I went back to New York. There were a lot of customers but not a lot of cheer in the bookstore. One of the customers had to remind Wendy to turn the Christmas music on.

Grace came in at her usual time but didn't stay long. I was helping a customer when she approached me. "I have my book," she said, lifting it from her tote to show me. I didn't even look to see what it was.

"I'll check you out as soon as I'm done here," I said.

"No hurry. I wrote everything down so someone can get to

it later. The counter was a little cluttered, so I left it attached to the notepad in the top drawer."

"Thank you."

"I probably won't get the chance to see you before Christmas. Or after, for that matter. I wanted to tell you that it's been a pleasure getting to know you better. You're an amazing young woman. I wish nothing but the best for you."

I felt emotional. "Thank you."

"I can see why your dad was so proud of you." She looked into my eyes for a moment, then said, "Merry Christmas, Noel. And have a happy birthday." She turned and walked out of the store. I wondered if I would ever see her again.

> *Dear Noel,*
> *Life is a house of cards balanced on a teeter-totter,*
> *precariously perched on a roller coaster. The only*
> *thing that should surprise us about our surprises is*
> *that we are surprised by them. Don't worry if life*
> *doesn't look the way you thought it would. It never*
> *does. Life is a ladder. You can choose the direction to*
> *climb, but not the rungs. As you climb, you will slip*
> *at times. Do not be discouraged. Sometimes success is*
> *better measured in intention than inches.*
>
> *Tabula Rasa*

CHAPTER

forty–eight

All great authors are seers.

—George Henry Lewes

WEDNESDAY, DECEMBER 23

I t snowed hard for most of the morning, not that it did much to deter our clientele. It was, after all, the last full shopping day before Christmas—the last chance at redemption for holiday procrastinators.

The day had been exhausting. Wendy was acting differently than she was yesterday. I don't know what it was. She almost acted as if nothing had happened. Perhaps it was the denial stage of grief. The two of us had worked a double shift, along with Cammy, Cyndee, and Teddy, our twenty-year-old tattooed rock star–wannabee holiday hire.

WendyflippedtheOPENsignovertoCLOSEDandlockedthedoor."One more day," she said. She handed me another letter. "This came today."

I was surprised to see it. "I guess this will be the last one."

"Why is that?"

Before I could answer, Teddy walked up behind us, his graffiti-covered army-surplus backpack slung over one shoulder. "Can I go now?"

Wendy nodded. "I'll see you tomorrow. Remember, we close early. Three o'clock."

"Peace out." He disappeared out the back.

"He's a funny kid," I said. "Good worker."

"He was," Wendy said, then added, "What a year. I wish your father had been here to see it all." She sighed. "No, I just wish he was here . . ." Her words trailed off in sadness.

For a moment neither of us spoke. Then she said, "Every Christmas Eve after we closed, your father and I would lock up and then go in back and have a celebratory glass of wine and just talk. I loved being with him." She seemed lost in the memory. A moment later she looked back at me as if suddenly awakened from a trance. "Are you spending tonight with Dylan?"

"No. We broke up."

Wendy looked at me quizzically. "I thought things were going well."

"They were. There was just . . . baggage, you know?" I lifted the envelope Wendy had just given me. "He won't admit that he's been writing the letters."

Wendy looked at me for a moment, then said, "He didn't write those letters."

"What?"

"They're from your father."

"How are they from my father? And that's definitely not his handwriting."

"It's Grace's handwriting. She's been sending them to you."

The casualness with which she shared this angered me. "If you knew all along, why didn't you tell me?"

"It wasn't my place to tell you. Your father was reaching out to you the only way he could get you to listen." She cocked her head to one side. "How did you not know they were from him? He wrote beautifully."

The revelation angered me. "Every time you talk about him, you sound like you were in love."

Wendy looked at me with amazement. "How can someone so smart be so dumb?" she said. "Of course I was in love with him. I always will be."

Her confession stunned me. I had meant the comment as a slight. I didn't really believe it was true. "Did he know how you felt?"

"Of course he did. We talked about it all the time. I wanted to marry him."

My thoughts spun more wildly. "What did he say to that?"

I could see anger rise in her eyes. "He said he couldn't take a wife that was his daughter's age. I told him that it didn't matter, but he said it would to you." Her eyes narrowed. "I said, 'Why do you care what she thinks? She doesn't care what you think. All she cares about is herself.' He didn't even dispute it. He just walked out. I had to call him and apologize." She shook her head. "And then he got sick."

Her eyes welled, and she wiped away a tear. "I was with your father almost every day since I was fifteen. I was with him *every* day since he got sick. I held him as he lay dying. And do you know what he worried the most about during his last hours? You. It was always you. And you don't even give a—" She stopped herself, her lip quivering. "His love to you was like giving pearls to swine. I think you're pathetic."

My face turned hot. All I could think to say was "You're fired."

An amused smirk crossed her face. "Listen, honey, I was only staying because your father asked me to."

She took her key ring from her pocket, unhooked her store keys, and set them on the counter. "Good luck tomorrow," she said facetiously. She walked to the front door, then suddenly stopped and looked around, likely for the last time.

It was only then that I fully realized what I had done. I had just banished her from her home. She turned back to me, her eyes wet and angry. "I stayed here to keep you from killing the thing he loved. But you kill everything you touch. I'm not surprised you lost your husband, your job, and now your boyfriend. You're so consumed with yourself that you spread pain everywhere you go. My only consolation is that you'll die alone." Then she turned, unlocked the front door, and walked out into the falling snow.

Her words stung. I walked to the door and opened it, then ran around the side to where she was unlocking her car. I wanted to say something cruel, something to rebut all she had said, but, pathetically, all that came out was "I don't know how to set the alarm."

She just shook her head as she got into her car and drove away.

CHAPTER

forty–nine

Words can be like X-rays if you use them properly—
they'll go through anything.
—*Aldous Huxley*

Wendy's departure had left me breathless. Even as angry as I was, I knew I had done something horrible. I locked the front door then walked over to the alarm. I studied it for a few minutes before deciding I was more likely to set it off than set it, so I decided to just leave it alone and hope no one robbed us.

I looked down at the envelope I was still holding. *There are things that need to be said*, my father had said before I came back to Utah. I guess he had found a way to say them after all. It seemed obvious now that the letters were from my father. He used to call himself a pocket philosopher. But Grace? Why would she have involved herself in this. And why hadn't she let on?

I remembered that I had a sample of Grace's writing in the front desk—the note she'd left for the book she had purchased that I still hadn't gotten around to entering. I took the note out from the drawer and set it on the counter.

I opened the letter I'd just received to compare the writing, but found that it was scrawled in different handwriting from the others. It was a little difficult to read, as the writing appeared frail and shaky. I glanced down at the bottom of the letter. This time, my father had signed his name. My guess was that he had written the letter from his deathbed.

October 28

My dearest Noel,

The December when you were almost five years old you asked me why Santa came down the chimney instead of using the front door. You were always delightfully inquisitive. I told you it was because not everyone believed in him, so if he didn't sneak in, they might miss the gifts he brought for them.

In writing these letters anonymously, I suppose I too have come down the chimney in hopes that your lack of belief in me might not get in the way of what I wished to share. Please forgive my dear friend Grace for following my wishes. I seek your forgiveness, not just for the subterfuge of these letters but for every way I have failed you. I ask this not for my sake but for yours. The weight of a parent's failures is much too heavy a burden for any child to carry. The ship must release the anchor for its own journey. My journey is over; yours has only begun.

Mark Twain wrote, "The two most important days in your life are the day you are born and the day you find out why." In this we share a day. The day you were born was the day I discovered why I was born. How grateful I am that you came into my life.

In the end, and, if this is, indeed, my end, remember this: Christmas is the story of a Father reaching out to His children. Nothing more. Nothing less.

This is me reaching out to you just one last time, my beloved daughter. It is my deepest hope that my words may help you in your journey ahead. I ask just one kindness in return, one small gift from you: Believe that you are loved by me and always were.

Your loving father,
Robert

My mind reeled. *Stop pretending that you loved me! You killed my mother and sent me away. Why are you tormenting me?* I wiped tears from my eyes, only to find them quickly replaced. After all this time, why was I suddenly unsure? And why was I holding so tightly to my pain?

CHAPTER

fifty

Let me live, love, and say it well in good sentences.

—Sylvia Plath

I still had several of the week's letters in my purse. I took the note that Grace had written to the back office, set it down on the desk, and then laid down next to it the last letter I'd received from Tabula Rasa. Grace's penmanship was highly stylistic. There was no doubt the handwriting was hers.

I looked up Grace's address in our customer records. I wrote it down, then went out in the storm to my car. My emotions felt as wild as the weather. I had no idea what I'd say, but I was going to confront her.

Grace lived in the Capitol Hill area, a wealthier section of Salt Lake City just north of the Salt Lake business district. I had suspected she was wealthy, and her neighborhood confirmed it. She lived in a gated community with well-spaced, stately homes.

I pulled my car up to the community's entrance, which required passing through security—a stucco-and-rock guard booth that had been decorated with Christmas lights and a large green wreath that framed a stop sign. The yellow-and-black-striped security gate that blocked the entrance was wrapped with silver tinsel garland and a sign reading HAPPY HOLIDAYS.

Inside the booth was a uniformed, badged security guard— a broad, muscular man with graying hair. I rolled down my window, and in spite of the booth's overhanging roof, snow-flakes fell inside my car. The security guard slid open his window, which was streaked on the inside from condensation. I could hear Christmas music coming from the booth. "May I help you?"

"I'm here to see Grace Kingsbury."

He glanced down at a clipboard, then back at me. "Is Ms. Kingsbury expecting you?"

"No. She doesn't know I'm coming. My name is Noel Post. I mean, Book. Noel Book."

The man looked at me doubtfully. "You sure?"

"Sorry. I'm not crazy. I just went through a divorce. I don't know what my last name is anymore."

"I'm sorry," he said, sounding sincere. "I understand." He lifted a brown phone receiver to his ear and dialed a number. I could hear him speaking. "This is Rich from security. There is a Miss Noel Book here to see you. Thank you. I'll let her in."

He set down the receiver and turned to me. "Do you know where Ms. Kingsbury lives?"

"No, sir."

"Take this street down to the corner and turn right. She's in the second home from the corner, number 227. There's cov-ered visitor parking across the street from her place."

"Thank you."

The security gate rose, and I quickly pulled forward to get

past it before it fell again. Following the guard's instructions, I parked across from her house.

Grace's home was an elegant French chateau–inspired mansion. It was probably four or five times larger than my father's home, with four chimneys and seven gables. It was covered with roughly textured French provincial brick and the large-paned windows on the ground floor were flanked by olive-green shutters that matched the oxidized, vacant copper planters beneath the higher windows. Even draped in snow, I could tell that the yard had been elaborately landscaped with the frosted outline of pruned shrubs and lines of columnar trees that were tied up in burlap sheets between occasional statuary. The heated cobblestone driveway was not only clear but dry.

Near the front of the home was a fountain that was covered for the winter. Directly behind the fountain was a glass-and-wrought-iron entryway surrounded by thick stone pillars and nestled beneath a second-story balcony. It looked like a home for nobility.

I walked up the cleared path to the door, unsure of what I would say, but my emotions were still growing in intensity. I rang the bell.

After the call from the guard, Grace was expecting me and almost immediately answered the door. She was dressed in jeans and a cashmere sweater that fell past her knees.

"Noel. I wasn't expecting to see you so soon." She looked down at the envelope in my hands. "I see you figured it out."

"How dare you?" I said.

"I dare a good many things," she said calmly. "To what are you specifically referring?"

"You wrote these letters."

"No, I transcribed them. Or penned them, if you prefer. But it was your father who wrote them."

"I don't care what you call it," I said. "You lied to me."

"I did no such thing."

"You withheld information."

"I withheld information," she repeated, shaking her head. "When did I do that?"

"When you didn't tell me."

"You never asked, dear. And I never offered. That doesn't make me a liar any more than it makes you an accomplice. More important, it's what your father desired."

"My father desired," I repeated angrily. "You're all such sycophants."

She smiled at the accusation. "I suppose we are. It's because we love him. My question is, why don't you? He certainly loved you."

"If you think that, you didn't know him."

"I think I knew your father better than you did."

I went straight for the jugular. "Then you knew he was abusive?"

To my surprise, Grace seemed more amused than shocked. "You're claiming that your father abused you?"

"Not me. My mother."

She still looked unimpressed. "Tell me about this abuse. Was it physical?"

I suddenly felt like I was on trial. "I was young. I don't remember."

"You must have some memory. At least enough to keep you bitter for all these years."

"The night my mother died he was holding her down. She was screaming at him to let her go."

"That's all you remember?"

"It's enough," I said. "It was traumatic."

Grace breathed out deeply, her eyelids falling slightly. "What else do you remember about that night?"

"More than I care to."

"Do you know how your mother died?"

"Of course I do. She died in a car accident."

"Do you know who was at fault in the accident?"

"My father."

For the first time Grace looked angry. "Your father wasn't in the car."

"I don't know. Probably my mother. She was upset. She was sobbing when she left the house."

Grace looked at me for a moment, then said, "How much do you really know about your mother?"

The way she framed the question angered me more. "Not as much as I'd like to. She was taken from me."

"And I'm guessing you'd like to keep it that way."

"What do you mean?"

"I mean that you don't really want to know the truth about your mother."

My temper flared. "My mother was a good woman. There's nothing you or my father's calumny can do to change that."

"*Calumny*," she repeated softly. "You inherited your father's love of words." She looked at me for a moment, then said, "Nevertheless, I have nothing more to share with you. So go on believing whatever you wish. Merry Christmas." She started to close the door.

I reached out to stop her. "Why are you doing this to me?"

"What do you think I'm doing to you?"

"You're tormenting me."

"No, dear, that's entirely your doing. I've done nothing but advocate for one of the finest men I will ever know. But, unlike your father, I don't suffer fools. And life has taught me that there are none so deaf as those who will not hear."

"What could you tell me that would change what happened?"

"Not a blessed thing. Nothing will change what happened. It will only change what you *believe* happened."

"Then tell me."

Grace hesitated as if she were deciding whether or not I was worthy of her time. "All right. Let's see how you do with truth. You're right, dear—your mother *was* a good woman. That is, when she wasn't drinking."

"What are you talking about?"

"Your mother was an alcoholic. It was a torment and a battle that your father fought with her. The night of the accident your mother had been drinking heavily, and, in spite of your father's efforts, she went out. That's why he was holding her down. That's why he blamed himself for not stopping her. She only made it a few miles before she crossed over the yellow line and hit an oncoming car head-on. That's how she died."

My head spun at the revelation. "If that's true, why didn't my father tell me?"

"Because you were young. Because he loved you," she said, the words falling carefully from her tongue. "He thought he was protecting you, even if it was at his expense."

"You're saying that he loved me so much he lied to me?"

"However you wish to frame it," she said. "He didn't want you to think of yourself as the daughter of an alcoholic. Or a murderer."

The word shook me. "My mother wasn't a murderer."

"Then a manslaughterer, if you find that more palatable." Her eyes darkened. "More than just your mother died that night. There were others. There were a man and his son in the other car, coming home from a high school basketball game. One the boy had just played in."

The explanation was more than I expected. "Is that the story my father told you?"

"I didn't need him to tell me." Suddenly her eyes welled up. It was the first time since my father's funeral that I had seen emotion on her face. "I wish I didn't know so much about it. God knows, I wish I didn't." Her eyes welled up. "Your father and I both lost our families that day."

It took me a moment to understand what she was saying. "Your husband and son were in the other car?"

She didn't need to answer.

"I'm sorry." It took me a moment to speak. "How did you become friends with my father?"

"I got to know him through the experience. He was as broken as I was. And he was so very sorrowful—not just for his own loss but mine as well. He blamed himself that he didn't stop her." She looked at me. "I came to his store every week to see him. And to be with him. Through time I came to care about him."

"If my mother was so bad, why didn't he just leave her?"

"It's not that simple, dear. Love's never that simple."

"But it probably would have been for the best."

"You're not the only one who thought that. Your father lost some of his closest friends over that very thing. Some even claimed he was the problem. They called him an enabler.

"The truth was, he just loved her too much, and he was a hopeless optimist. He believed his love could save her." She looked down a moment, then said, "Maybe he just loved her too much to see the truth."

"What truth?"

"She had to love herself, too."

CHAPTER

fifty-one

Words are a lens to focus one's mind.

—Ayn Rand

There was nothing more to be said. As the silence stretched into further discomfort, Grace said, "I'm sorry I had to be the one to share this. But it's time you knew the truth. It's good to know the truth."

"Thank you," I said softly.

"If you need anything, you know where I live. Merry Christmas, Noel."

I drove home in silence, the only sound coming from the blowing of the car heater and the flapping of the windshield wipers. I had the letter from my father on the seat next to me. My mind reeled through a labyrinth of emotions. I reimagined the scene I'd played out in my mind ten thousand times, of my father holding down my screaming mother, but now with new understanding. He was trying to save her life.

My neighborhood was quiet, the homes glowing with the festive colors of Christmas in contrast to my house, which was dark inside and out.

I turned on the kitchen light, then turned up the heat. I hadn't had anything to eat since lunch, but I was too upset to eat or to make anything. I poured myself a glass of wine, then sat at the kitchen table and again took the letter out of the envelope, laying it out to read. The cuckoo chirped the half hour.

> *In writing these letters anonymously, I suppose I too have come down the chimney in hopes that your lack of belief in me might not get in the way of what I wished to share.*

It was just as Grace had said; there are none so blind as those who will not see. I had been willingly walking blind for decades. *What do you do when you realize that your life has been a lie?* I read the letter again. And again.

I looked at the date my father had scrawled at the top of the letter. October 28. It took me a moment to realize that the date couldn't be right, as he'd died October 27, the day I'd arrived back in Utah. Maybe, in his state, he'd been confused about the date.

As I examined the date more closely—and the numbers around it—I noticed something about my father's handwriting. The date wasn't October 28, it was actually October 18. I remembered Wendy complaining about my father's handwriting—especially his numbers. She had said that his ones looked like twos.

I went to my room and grabbed the paper on which he'd written the safe's combination.

23 R – 32 L – 52 R

The first 2 looked different than the others. It looked just like the 1 on his letter. I'd been dialing the wrong number.

I rewrote the combination.

13 R– 32 L – 52 R

I sat down at the safe and carefully turned the dial. This time it clicked at the last number. I felt as if I were opening a time capsule. I suppose I was. My heart pounded as I slowly opened the door.

The first thing I saw was a small round ring dish. I had made it in school in the second grade as a Father's Day gift. Our class had sculpted the pieces in clay, and our teacher had them fired and glazed so we could paint them.

I held it up to examine it. I hadn't seen it since I was a child, and it brought back a flood of memories. Written on the bottom were my words in a seven-year-old's earnest script:

Happy Father s Day

I thought parents just threw these things away. But here it was among his most precious possessions.

Next to the dish were a pair of pink ballet slippers. My first dance shoes. They were tied together by their silk ribbons. I took them out. I remembered how special I felt wearing them. I set them down next to the dish.

Under the shoes was a small square unsealed envelope. I extracted the contents. The message was scrawled in crayon in a child's handwriting.

Happy Burth day,
I lov lov lov U.
Yor DoTTer
NOEL

I smiled. I was only four when I wrote that. I especially loved that I felt the need to remind him that I was his "Dotter." Next to the letter was a more formal piece of stationery, a crimson envelope. The outside had just two words written in soft, feminine handwriting:

My Dearest

I pulled back the flap and took out the letter. There were tear stains on the paper. Whether they were from the writer or the recipient, I don't know. Maybe both. I began to read.

My beloved Robert,
How do you still hold to me? How do you continue to hope beyond hope?
The bigger question on my heart is Why? Why do you still believe in me after all my failures? I want to believe I can be your butterfly, that this earthbound caterpillar can emerge from the cocoon of her shame and fly. I want to believe I can be that

*transcendent creature you believe I can be—the one
only you can see.*

*But I can't, my love. It's time we accept this. I
can't beat this, Robert. God knows I've tried. The
only thing worse than losing you and my daughter
would be to fail you both again. Please don't let
me. Please let me go. Please let me disappear like
a stone dropped in the sea. Let me sink alone into
the darkness. You must leave me, dearest. For your
and our Noel's sake. What life can she hope for as
you cling to me? She deserves better than I can give
her. You deserve better. You believe in me too much,
my beloved. Not everyone is as strong as you. I beg
you, please stop believing in me. Let me go. Let me
sink.*

> *Your unworthy,*
> *Celeste*

Still clutching the letter, I wiped my eyes with my forearm.
Two of my own tears fell onto the page, adding to the others.

What Grace had said about my mother was true. I knew it
when she said it, but here was evidence from my mother herself. How had my father dealt with such pain? I checked the
date to see when the letter had been written. It was dated just
two days before her death.

I wiped my eyes again and looked deeper into the safe.

Next to my mother's letter was another envelope, only this
one had my name on it, written in my father's handwriting.
There was something in the envelope as well. I tore it open.

There was a letter and a pearl bracelet with a yellow-gold clasp. The pearls were iridescent cream and spherical. I took the letter from the envelope.

> *My dear Noel,*
> *If you're reading this letter, I am gone. I bought*
> *this bracelet for your wedding in the off chance you*
> *changed your mind and invited me to the ceremony. I*
> *hoped to give it to you the night before your wedding,*
> *to speak to you lovingly as a father speaks to his*
> *daughter at such a time. As heartbroken as I am, I*
> *honor your wish not to include me. But I was there,*
> *if not in person, then in the shadows of my heart. I'm*
> *sure your mother was there as well. I also purchased*
> *for you a Lladró figurine of a bride. I will keep it here*
> *until you someday claim it with all the rest.*
>
> *I saw pictures of you from your wedding posted*
> *online. You were as beautiful as any bride who has ever*
> *walked the earth. As beautiful even as your mother. I*
> *have written a small book about that day. It's called* The
> Dance, *and it's about us. I have kept the only copy of it*
> *in this safe. What you choose to do with it is up to you.*
>
> *I am sorry that I offended you in questioning your*
> *choice of partners. I was only trying to protect you. I*
> *should have been more sensitive. In all my life I have never*
> *hoped so much to be wrong. I hope I was wrong about*
> *him and that he loves you even as I do. This is my hope.*
>
> *Love,*
> *Dad*

I wiped my eyes again. "You weren't wrong, Dad," I said. "I should have listened. I was too prideful." I put the bracelet on. It was beautiful. It would have perfectly accented my wedding dress. Part of me was glad it hadn't been part of that day, to be downgraded with the rest of the memories of that failed relationship. I had already thrown away my dried bouquet and sold my dress.

There was more to the letter.

> P.S. One can never be fully certain of the results of one's choices, only one's intention. I may have been wrong to send you away to that school in Tucson, but my intentions weren't. The day I came home and found you drinking, I saw history repeating itself. I didn't see you on the ground, Noel, I saw your mother, and I was there when they carried her body from the wreckage.
> If you don't know by now, your mother was an alcoholic, as her mother too was an alcoholic, as was her grandfather. Some families seem to be wired that way. As her daughter, I knew you might carry the same wiring. I failed your mother by letting her out of the house that night. Others, innocent people, were hurt by my failure. I couldn't take that chance with you. You might hate me for my decision, but I am grateful that you are alive to hate me. I take consolation in that.

I looked inside the safe for the book my father had written about in his letter. It was thin and lay flat against the back of the safe. I brought it out. On the cover was the picture of a little girl dancing alone in a field of flowers. The title read:

THE DANCE
by Robert Book

I took the book over to my father's bed and lay down to read. I opened it to the dedication page.

For Noel.
Never stop dancing.

I wiped a tear from my cheek, then began to read.

A father once had a daughter.

She was a happy little girl who liked the things that little girls do—dress-ups and kittens and sometimes both together. But most of all she liked to dance.

Nearly every day she would jump and spin in the thick, wild grass near the edge of the yard where the tall meadow flowers grew. Though she didn't see him, her father watched.

And he smiled.

When the girl was old enough to go to school, she danced in the Thanksgiving play, dressed as an ear of corn. She could not see out of her costume very well and tripped over a boy dressed as a carrot. Though she could not see her father, he was watching.

And he smiled.

When the girl was a little older, she took dance lessons. She wore a pink tutu and soft leather ballet slippers. At her first recital she tried very hard to remember her steps. She did not see her father standing close to the stage.

But he was smiling.

A few years later the girl became a graceful ballerina. She wore pink satin toe shoes with long shiny ribbons. One year she danced a solo in *The Nutcracker*. Everyone clapped when she finished. The crowd was large, and the stage lights were bright so the girl could not see her father in the audience. But he clapped louder than everyone else.

And he smiled wider than everyone else.

The girl grew into a young woman. One spring night she put on a beautiful gown and high-heeled pumps and went to her first prom with a young man. When the young man brought her home, they did not see her father peeking out the window as they slow-danced on the front porch.

(He wasn't smiling.)

The young woman fell in love with the young man and soon decided to marry. At the end of the wedding day she waltzed with her father. Then the father gave his girl's hand to the young man and left the dance floor. As the young woman gazed into her new husband's eyes, she did not see her father watching from the side of the room.

Though the father's eyes were moist, he smiled.

The young woman and her new husband moved far away from the home with the thick grass and tall meadow flowers. Whenever he missed his daughter, the father would take out an old shoebox filled with photographs of her dancing. As he looked at the pictures, he remembered each dance.

And he smiled.

Many years passed.

One day the father called his daughter on the telephone. "I am old now. I am cold and very tired," he said. "Please come to me. I would like to see you dance just one more time."

The daughter came. She found her father in his bed. And she danced for him.

But the father did not smile.

"I cannot see you," he said. "My eyes are not much good. Dance close to the bed so I can hear your feet." The woman walked close to the bed, then she jumped and spun as she had as a little girl.

The father smiled.

Then the woman sat on her father's bed. She lay her face against his, took his hand, and they swayed back and forth. In this way, they danced once more.

"I have danced many times," the woman whispered into her father's ear, "in many places and for many people. But I have always danced for you. How can I ever dance again?" She buried her head in her father's chest.

But her father shook his head. "You must never stop dancing," he said. "For though you will not see me, whenever you dance, I will be watching."

Then the father went to sleep.

As the daughter sadly left his side, she stopped at the doorway and looked back once more at the father she loved. And then she danced. And though she could not see him, her father was watching.

And he smiled.

How could I have been so wrong? Not just about my father, but about everything? I had lived my life as a victim of false narratives demonizing those who loved me most, blaming them for my choices. There was nothing left to defend. My life was one big lie.

All I could do was weep. It seemed that that was all I had

done for most of the day, but there was something deeper about these tears, as if they had been squeezed from the very core of my being. I lay back in my father's bed as wave after wave of sadness washed over me. All I could say was, "I'm so sorry, Daddy." I fell asleep clutching the book to my chest.

CHAPTER

fifty–two

Books have that strange quality, that being of the frailest and tenderest matter, they outlast brass, iron, and marble.

—William Drummond

THURSDAY, CHRISTMAS EVE

I woke the next morning with the sun streaming through the blinds in my father's room. I looked around, temporarily forgetting where I was. The closet was open, as was the safe. My father's book lay on the floor. I was fully dressed.

I looked down at my watch. It was five minutes after nine. I was late for work. *At least Wendy's there to open the store*, I thought. Then I remembered that I'd fired her. I jumped out of bed and hurriedly got dressed, grabbing a brush to comb my hair on the way in to the bookstore.

It was nearly nine thirty when I arrived. There was a line of almost twenty people standing out in the cold, two of whom were my Christmas employees Teddy, from the day before, and Marcia, whom I'd met only once.

I parked in my spot. I had never gotten a key to the back door—I'd never needed one, since Wendy was always here first—so I had to walk around to the front, past the disgruntled crowd, apologizing the whole way. "I'm here, I'm so sorry. I'm here."

"There's a line here," a gruff voice shouted at me.

"I own the place!" I shouted back.

"Then why are you late?"

"Bob was never late," someone else said.

"New management," the gruff voice said sarcastically.

"Where's Wendy?" a woman asked as I fumbled through my keys. "She's not answering her phone."

"She's not coming in today," I said as I unlocked the door, the crowd pressing in around me. "Back up, please."

"But I talked to her yesterday," the woman said. "She said she'd be here."

"Well, she won't. Something came up."

"Wendy's not here?" another customer asked.

This created a ripple effect in the line not unlike the telephone game. "Did she say Wendy's not going to be here?" "Wendy quit?" "Wendy's sick?" "What does she have?" "Is she in the hospital?"

I walked into the store. It was dark and cold, not the usual ambience I'd grown accustomed to. I realized that I had never even turned on the lights before. It was an older building, and the switches weren't where any normal human would expect them. As people began crowding into the dark store, I shouted, "Does anyone know how to turn on the lights?"

"I'll get them," Teddy said, brushing by me, using his phone as a flashlight. He walked to the back.

"I thought you were the owner," someone behind me said.

"She's no Bob," someone else said.

No, I'm not, I said to myself.

The lights went on. By that point I was ready to kick everyone out, but I think they probably would have just looted the store. Teddy walked out from the back. "The alarm wasn't set last night."

"I know the alarm wasn't set."

"No worries," he said. "We weren't robbed."

"Would you turn on some Christmas music, please?" I asked.

"Will do, boss," he said.

A tall woman wearing a fur-lined, plaid trapper hat buttoned beneath her chin walked up to me. Her cheeks were red as though she'd spent too much time outdoors. "Wendy set aside some books for me."

I looked around the counter. I couldn't see them. "I'll find them. What's your name?"

"Maria."

"Maria what?"

"Wendy knew."

"I'm not Wendy!" I shouted.

She looked at me for a moment, then said, "Clearly."

Someone just shoot me.

The next six hours passed by like an eternity. We had more than a hundred customers, all rushing to grab last-minute gifts before heading to their gatherings. It seemed that everyone had somewhere to be except me.

As the owner, I should have been happy about all the business, but I wasn't. I felt disassociated from it all, with the holiday, the spirit, even the store. I was unworthy to stand in this place. Wendy was right—I killed everything I touched. I was misery personified.

It was ten minutes after three. Teddy had locked the front door, and I was helping our last customer—a young, frantic woman who had run in just a few minutes before closing to pick up a couple of books. They were gifts for her children. Her credit card kept being declined. After several attempts I finally said, "I'm sorry. This card isn't going through. Do you have another card? Or cash?"

The woman looked flustered. "No. There should still be some money on there."

I tried the card again, only to have it be declined again. I could sense her embarrassment. I exhaled slowly. "Just take them."

"What?"

"Just take the books. They're on me. Merry Christmas."

She looked at me in disbelief. "Really?" To my surprise, tears welled up in her eyes. "I've been out of work for two months. You don't know how much this helps. Thank you. God bless you."

"You're welcome." I let her out of the store, then relocked the door after her.

Behind me someone said, "That was mighty decent."

I turned around. Teddy was standing there. "Her card wasn't working."

"I saw what happened. You could tell she didn't have the money and you helped her out. You're a good person."

I didn't know what to say. I felt like anything but a good person. "Thank you."

"Boss, if you don't need anything else, I'm going to head out."

"You can go."

"Thanks. Wait, forgot something." He ran out of the room, then came back wearing his pack. "Hey, I don't know if I ask you or Wendy, but are you hiring after Christmas? I'd like to work here. I love its vibe, you know? It's a cool place."

He just stood there looking at me hopefully.

"Thanks, Teddy. I don't know if we're hiring yet. Check with me next week."

"Okay. Thanks. Peace out. Merry Christmas." He walked out of the store.

I walked over and turned off the Christmas music and the front window lights. The light outside had already diminished, and the snow was falling hard, coating the world in a silent blue-white batting.

In the silence and stillness of the moment, I looked around the store. For the first time I saw it. My father was all around me. In the books, the shelves, the million details he had created over the decades of care. The bookstore was sacred ground, not just to him, but to the people who loved him. It was my father's temple, the consolidation of his wisdom, wit, and spirit—the totality of his ponderings in a world that the rest of us were trying to make sense of.

Inexplicably, my father had made sense of it all. Somehow, through the tragedy and loss and pain, he never wavered from his optimism. With all the world's cruelty and hypocrisy, he never gave up hope in humanity. Not even in his daughter. No, especially not in his daughter. In the face of my anger and bitterness, his love never quit.

No wonder so many people loved him. And the bookstore was his gathering place for those he loved—a keep and a bulwark against the storms and waves of despair and ignorance. It's no wonder Wendy had fought to keep the bookstore alive. She was keeping *him* alive.

I took the money out of the register and put it in the safe. Then I locked up the store and walked out alone.

CHAPTER

fifty–three

I am irritated by my own writing. I am like a violinist whose ear is true but whose fingers refuse to reproduce precisely the sound he hears within.

—Gustave Flaubert

For nearly half an hour I sat in my car with tears streaming down my cheeks. I was grateful for the snow falling, blanketing me, further insulating me from the world I feared. Everything Wendy had said about me was true. I was pathetic. I deserved to be alone. And, like she said, I would someday die alone. I had blamed the world for my unhappiness, but there was no one to blame but myself. Dylan had reached out in love, and I had used that love to punish him for daring to care.

For the first time in my life, I wanted to be held accountable. The only one I could think would do it was Grace.

I made my way downtown through deserted streets back to her home. The same man was at the security booth from the night before. I could see that the counter inside the booth was covered with fruit baskets and presents, likely given to the man by residents coming back from work or parties.

To my surprise, the man remembered me. "Merry Christmas, young lady. Is it Miss Post or Miss Book today?"

"You pick this time."

He laughed. "Let's go with Miss Book. You're here for Ms. Kingsbury again?"

"Yes, sir."

"Just a moment." He lifted his phone. "Ms. Kingsbury, Miss Book is here to see you again. Thank you. I'll send her through. And a Merry Christmas to you too."

He turned to me. "There're a lot of visitors tonight, so you can park along the street if you have to. You won't be towed. It's the one night of the year we allow that."

"Thank you," I said. "Have a Merry Christmas."

"You too. And a happy New Year."

I drove around the corner to Grace's house. The visitor parking spots were all taken, so I parked along the curb and got out.

Grace opened the door before I could ring the bell. Her hair was perfectly coiffed, and she was dressed beautifully, in a deep maroon dress with gold piping and a large holly-shaped brooch of emeralds and rubies.

"You look nice," I said. "You must have a party."

"I'm a little early, but I have Midnight Mass," she said. She looked at me kindly. "What can I do for you, dear?"

As I looked at her, my eyes suddenly filled with tears. "I have no place to go. I have no one."

She stepped forward and put her arms around me. "You have me," she said. "You've come to the right place."

CHAPTER

fifty-four

Writing is like driving at night in the fog. You can only see as far as your headlights, but you can make the whole trip that way.

—E. L. Doctorow

The last time I'd been to Grace's house I hadn't gotten past the front door—let alone my emotions—so I hadn't really seen her home. It was exquisitely designed, with cream-and-gold fabric paneling and marble floors with plush, gold-fringed rugs. There was art everywhere, beautiful quality pieces like I had seen in the galleries in New York.

"Come in here," she said. She led me to a spacious front room. The ceiling was high, at least twelve feet, with coffered ceilings framing a large crystal chandelier. In the corner was a Christmas tree that almost reached the ceiling, intricately decorated with twinkling lights and small, feathered birds, satin ribbons, and clear amber and purple glass baubles the size of grapefruits.

"Please have a seat."

"Thank you," I said. "You have a beautiful home."

She smiled. "Thank you."

"You don't have visitors tonight?"

She looked at me gently. "No. I don't have any family."

"My mother took your family away."

"That was a long time ago, Noel. We'll let the spirit of Christmas Past tend to her own. Agreed?"

I nodded.

"I hope you're hungry. You're just in time for dinner."

"I didn't come for . . ."

"It's okay, dear. As you can see, I've already set the table for two." She motioned to an adjacent dining room. Candles glowed from a holiday centerpiece.

"How did you know I was coming?"

"I didn't. The place was set for your father. We spent every Christmas Eve together. I'm a creature of habit, and it was my way of inviting him back. Or denying that I lost my best friend." She looked at me sadly. "Then again, maybe he sent you."

"My father came here on Christmas Eve?"

"Every Christmas Eve." Her face lit with a fond smile. "Such beautiful times we had. The stories your father would tell over a hot buttered rum."

"My father didn't drink."

"He did on occasion. He did on Christmas Eve. With me." She smiled. "I guess that's not all true. We'd also toast the New Year with a Dom Perignon. Sometimes a Möet & Chandon. For a man who didn't drink he had a surprisingly sophisticated palate."

"You spent the holidays with my father?"

"Always."

"Did Wendy know?"

Grace laughed; it was a sweet, full expulsion. "So you know about Wendy?"

"She told me."

"She's a very beautiful young woman. She was quite smitten with your father. Of course, so was I. Two women in love with the same man. What's a woman to do?" Her brows rose. "What's a man to do?"

"He was lucky," I said.

"We were the lucky ones."

"I fired Wendy yesterday."

Grace looked at me in surprise. "Oh my. What on earth drove you to that?"

I looked at her and said, "I'm an idiot."

Grace burst out laughing. "Oh good, you're finally being honest. It makes life so much easier. Pretense is such a burden. The day I accepted that beneath my pristine, polished surface I was a broken hot mess was the day my life became manageable." She leaned forward. "Your father saw through my veneer like it was glass. He showed me that what was behind it was a lot more interesting."

"Did he spend every Christmas Eve with you?"

"For the last fifteen years. After he closed up his shop, he'd spend a little time with Wendy, then he'd come on up."

"Wendy told me that. At least, about her. I'm surprised you knew."

"Your father was terribly honest. I don't think I ever caught him in a lie." She suddenly smiled. "Unless it was a kind lie. So, after his little visit with Wendy, he'd come here and I'd make him a very special dinner. I'm quite the cook, you know, though not as good as your father made me out to be. The way he spoke, you'd think I was a Michelin-rated chef.

"We'd have his personal favorite, Beef Wellington with Parma ham and puff pastry, candied carrots, Potatoes Dauphinoise, asparagus with hollandaise sauce. He would bring the wine and cheesecake. The cheesecake he ordered from New York. I don't remember the name, but it was Zagat-rated number one."

"S&S," I said.

"Yes, that's it. Your father had remarkable taste in books and food and wine."

"And people," I said.

She smiled. "In everything. Probably why we got along so well." She sighed. "I miss him."

"I miss him too," I said. It was the first time I'd said that out loud since I left Utah. I think Grace understood that, and she let my confession fall into silence.

"We would dine for hours. Then, after we ate, we'd go to Midnight Mass together." She looked at me for a moment, then said, "Would you like to go with me to mass tonight?"

"I've never been." I looked down at my clothes. "I'm not really dressed for it."

"You look fine. I always overdress. It's just me."

"I'd like to," I said.

She smiled. "I thought I would be going alone this year for the first time. What a pleasant turn of events."

The dinner was as exquisite as my father had once voiced. So was my host. I never sensed that I was intruding on Grace's evening; rather, she treated me as a long-awaited guest—one she had been looking forward to entertaining.

A little after eleven we took her car, a candy-apple-red Cadillac, and drove to mass at the Cathedral of the Madeleine on South Temple Street. It was only a few miles from her home.

We were early for the service and in no great hurry. I was handed a program by a robed child near the entrance, and Grace and I took a seat near the center of the cathedral.

I had never been religious-minded, but the smell of incense, the glowing candles, and the pageantry filled me with peace. As I looked over the program Grace said, "Don't worry about a thing. There's a lot of singing and kneeling. Just follow my lead. No one's watching to see if you do it right." She smiled. "Or wrong."

"Will there be some kind of communion?"

"Yes. But you're not Catholic, so you don't need to participate."

"Are you Catholic?"

"Twice a year," she said with a wry smile.

The choir-led music was beautiful and familiar, and I found myself recklessly joining in it all. There was a gospel reading, followed by the homily. Fittingly, the priest spoke of God's great love as an analogy for a father's love. The service ended with a presentation by bell ringers playing "I Heard the Bells on Christmas Day."

We filed out of the cathedral past a short receiving line, and then we walked back to the car. As we drove back to Grace's home, she said, "Thank you for coming with me, Noel. What a beautiful evening this has turned out to be."

"It's been nice," I said. "Not at all what I planned on."

"Call me a romantic, but I really believe your father sent me a replacement. He must be so pleased."

When we got back, there was a different security guard in the booth. "Merry Christmas, Michael," Grace said, stopping her car.

"Merry Christmas, Mrs. Kingsbury," he returned.

"I have something for you." She reached into her purse and handed him a fifty-dollar bill. "Merry Christmas. Don't stay up too late."

He laughed. "Too late for that. Thank you, Mrs. Kingsbury."

As we pulled into her garage, she said, "I know it's late, but please come in for just a few minutes. I think there are still a few things to be said."

I followed her inside. She took off her coat and scarf and folded them over the back of a sofa. "Can I send any food home with you?"

"I'm okay," I said.

"Please, have a seat."

I sat back down on the sofa. Grace came over and sat next to me.

"Now that you know the truth, how do you feel?"

Suddenly my eyes welled up. "I hurt. My father loved me, and I repaid him with hate."

"You didn't hate your father, Noel. You were a child. Your mother died and it didn't make sense to you, and you were looking for a place to put all that pain. Something to blame. Or some*one*. I understand that. I went through it myself, and I was an adult. Some people choose to blame God. You chose to blame the man you loved most. Your father understood that. I know because we talked about it."

"But where do I go with that? I can't tell him I'm sorry."

She took my hand. "It's not as difficult as you think." She looked softly into my eyes. "Your father believed this day would come. I have no doubt that he's smiling down on you right now. He was never looking for an apology, Noel. He was just hoping you would come home, even if just in your heart. And here you are."

"But it's too late."

"No," she said. "It's never too late. And there is still something you can do for him."

"I'll do anything."

"Answer me this. What is it that your father desired most?"

I rubbed my eyes. "I don't know."

"Yes, you do, Noel. Don't be afraid to say it. What did your father want most of all? In all his actions toward you, what's the one common thread that ran through everything?"

I suddenly understood. "He wanted me to be happy."

A broad smiled crossed her face. "Exactly. So does your unhappiness serve his desire?"

"No."

"Exactly." She looked into my eyes. "If you wish to honor him, give him what he wanted most. Be happy. Not for your sake, but for his."

My eyes filled with tears. Grace put her arms around me and held me. After a minute she said, "Oh, there's one more thing—one more wish he had. I'll be right back." She left the room, returning a moment later carrying a cardboard box. She set it on the table.

"You know, your father followed your writing religiously. He commented on your editing and the effect you had on your authors. He was brilliant that way. He read every book you edited. He knew every one of your authors and read their books."

"Even Jerica Bradley?"

She grinned. "Not exactly high art, but even Jerica Bradley." She rubbed her hand down my arm. "You once asked me what book I put in his casket. I didn't answer you, because you weren't ready. But you are now. The book was called *The Silent Heart*."

"I've never heard of it."

"That's because it was never published. Your father wrote it. It was one of the most beautiful books I have ever read. It wasn't just beautifully written, but it was beautiful in its depth and message. I believe it could have been a candidate for the National Book Award. Of course, your father didn't care about such trivial things. He was a true artist. He used to say, 'The purest work must be created for the eyes of God alone.' And, fortunately, my eyes. I was the only one who read his book. It was a tremendous honor. He only printed one copy, then erased the manuscript. He wanted it buried with him."

"It's gone?"

"Like him," she said. "I know, I probably shouldn't have done it, but it was a promise he made me make. Trust me, I've doubted what I did since they closed the casket, but it's done now." She looked deeply into my eyes. "Your father's secret hope was that he would someday be able to write a book with you."

Her words brought more pain. "Just another way I've failed him."

She smiled. "No, you haven't." She gestured to the box on the table. "That's why I brought this in. Your father left two books for you to finish. If you really want to know your father, finish his books. He lives in them."

I walked over to the table. "May I see them?"

"Of course," she said. "They're yours."

I lifted the cover off the box. The first page I saw had the words 'Title to Come.' I read the first page of the manuscript. "This is really good."

"Finish it, Noel. It was his fondest hope."

I put the page back and closed the box. "I don't know if I'm up to it."

"He thought you were," she said. "And I'm certain he'll collaborate with you. Every writer has a muse."

"Thank you." We embraced. "Thank you for everything."

"It's been my pleasure. And I do hope we have a standing date for next Christmas Eve. I hate to think of spending it alone for the rest of my life."

"It's a date," I said.

I lifted the box, and she watched as I carried it out to my snow-covered car. When I was halfway down the walk she suddenly shouted, "Oh, Noel."

I turned back. "Yes?"

"For God's sake, give Wendy her job back."

I laughed. "I'm on it."

CHAPTER

fifty-five

Long lay the world in sin and error pining,
Till He appeared and the soul felt its worth.
A thrill of hope, the weary world rejoices,
For yonder breaks a new and glorious morn.
Fall on your knees!
O hear the angel voices!
O night divine,
O night when Christ was born

It was my birthday. I woke with a song from the mass playing in my head: "O Holy Night." When I was young my father would replace that last refrain with my name. Maybe it's sacrilegious, but he'd celebrate my birthday by singing, "O night when Noel was born."

I had incredibly painful memories of Christmases without my mother, especially the year I lost her, but I had let them eclipse the many, many fond ones we'd shared.

Not this morning. While my heart ached for all I'd lost, there was also a sweetness for what I'd found. For the first time in years I didn't feel so incredibly alone. I felt light and hopeful. As the song said, "a thrill of hope." Truth had entered my heart, and just like that I was born again. And with that renaissance came purpose. I had things to do.

I went to my father's stationery drawer and took out a sheet of his most beautiful paper. I took it to the kitchen table and wrote a letter to my father—something I should have done years earlier. I put the finished letter in an envelope, then showered and got ready for the day. There were people I needed to see.

I opened the front door and was braced by the cold fresh air. The homes up and down my street were quiet. The only sign of life was a plume of smoke rising from the chimney of the house across the street.

My first stop was the cemetery. Except for an old Volkswagen minivan a few streets over from me, I was alone. The stark white of the cemetery was accented by the offerings left behind from earlier visitors: the bright crimson leaves of poinsettias and the evergreen of wreaths.

The snow I walked through was nearly up to my knees. When I got to my parents' grave, I cleared away a small patch of snow, exposing the wet, matted grass beneath, then knelt.

For a moment I just kneeled there, silently, and then I reached out and touched the stone, tracing the grooved letters of my father's name with my finger.

"Hi, Mom and Dad, it's Noel." I stopped talking. The words didn't come. I bowed my head as tears fell down my cheek. *Just be*, I thought.

"You probably didn't expect to see me today, but here I am. I'm just so glad you're finally together again." I wiped my eyes. "I'm glad I'm your daughter."

The tears rolled down my face. "Mom, I need to talk to Dad for a minute, okay?" I cleared my throat. "Daddy, I'm so sorry I was such a bad daughter. I didn't know what really happened that night or why you sent me away. That's not an excuse; maybe it's a reason." I bit my quivering lip. "If you were here, I'd hug you and tell you how sorry I am. I'd try to make up for all the things we missed out on. But you're not here.

"I'm going to try to keep you alive through all the things you loved. Your writing, your bookstore, your friends. I promise I'll do everything I can to keep them alive. And I'm sorry about Wendy. I'll take care of that too." I again wiped my tears. "I'm sorry, Daddy. I didn't know you were loving me all along. I know that now."

"I wrote a letter for you. Just like you wrote for me. I'll read it."

> *Dear Daddy,*
> *Even though I never deserved it, I was always*
> *your angel. Now you are mine. I will forever*
> *honor your memory and try to be the girl you*
> *believed I could be.*
>
> > *Love, your daughter,*
> > *Noel*

I put the letter back in the envelope and set it on the grave. "I love you, Daddy." I bowed my head and cried, the sounds muffled by the soft snow.

I don't remember how long I was there. It was a while.

Long enough that I was shivering and covered in snow. Still, I didn't even notice the cold. I wiped my eyes and was about to stand when something fluttered down past me. I thought it was a leaf until it lit on my parents' stone. Stark against the frigid backdrop of white was a blue butterfly.

CHAPTER

fifty–six

Words do not express thoughts very well. They always become a little different immediately after they are expressed, a little distorted, a little foolish.

—*Hermann Hesse*

A fter the cemetery, I drove to the bookstore. "Bob-books," I said out loud. "What a great name."

I had three reasons to visit the store. The first was to surround myself with my father's presence, to feel him again. The second was more practical: I needed to pick up a few Christmas presents. The third was to find Wendy's address.

I picked out three books and a candle and wrapped them. I put together another little package for Wendy, then searched for her address. It was harder to find than I thought it would be. I finally found it printed on her desk on a label for some makeup she'd ordered. She lived on the west side of the valley, about twenty minutes from the store by way of the interstate. She was my first stop.

My GPS led me west through a labyrinth of tract homes in an older, established suburb. As the sun rose higher on the day, life began to spring from the frozen world. I passed a small hill with children sledding and throwing snowballs.

Wendy lived on the crossroads of Emerson and Thoreau, which I figured had likely influenced her choice of neighborhoods. There were cars parked all along the curbs. Most of them seemed to have been there for a while, as they looked more like igloos than automobiles. The homes in the area were simple, mostly split-level and outdated—a sharp contrast to Grace's mansion.

I found Wendy's house number on a curbside mailbox, parked my car, and got out. The street was deserted, and the only sound was the whine of an unseen snowblower in the distance.

Wendy's front walk was covered with snow. Her home looked still and dark as if no one was home, but her Subaru was in the driveway.

I walked up to the door and rang the bell. After a moment I knocked. I heard some footsteps, followed by some fiddling with a chain lock and then the deadbolt. The door opened.

Wendy was wearing yoga pants and a sweatshirt. I don't know if her expression was more of disbelief or disgust, but she definitely wasn't happy to see me. She started to shut the door.

I put out my hand. "Wait, please."

"What do you want?"

"We need to talk."

"It's my day off," she said.

"Please. It's important."

"To who?"

"To my father," I said.

She leaned against the door frame, her arms crossed at her chest.

"I came to apologize."

"Why? Because you realized you can't run the store without me?"

"That's not why I came."

"Why would I believe you?"

"I brought you something." I handed her a small wrapped box. She reluctantly took the gift.

"Open it. Please."

She glanced at me suspiciously, then unwrapped the box and lifted its lid. Inside was her key to the store. She shook her head. "Does this mean you're giving me my job back?"

"No. It means I'm giving you the bookstore."

Her expression froze. "What?"

"I'm giving you the bookstore."

"Are you serious?"

"Would I lie about that?"

"It's more likely than you giving me the store." She looked into my eyes. "Why?"

"My father loved you. And it was something you two had together. He would have wanted it that way."

She looked at me for a moment, then said, "It's cold out; why don't you come in?"

"If I'm not disturbing anything."

"It's just me," she said.

I stomped the snow off my feet and walked into the house. Her front room was tidy, with colorful giclée prints. In one corner there was a small plastic Christmas tree sparsely decorated with frosted pinecones and gold baubles.

On two of the walls were framed pictures of Wendy with my father. In one of them, they were standing next to each other at a book signing with author Mary Higgins Clark. The picture was signed by Mary. The other photograph was of just the two of them in the canyons, the leaves behind them radiant in autumn colors. They looked deliriously happy.

"We took that one a year ago last fall," Wendy said.

"He looks happy. You both do."

"It was four months before he was diagnosed. It was our last hike."

I sat down on one of the couches. "You have a nice home."

"Thank you." She sat on a wooden chair next to the couch. One of her cats ran into the room and hopped up onto her lap.

"Which one is that?" I asked.

Wendy lifted the cat's chin. "It's Clawdia. She's the friendly one." Wendy rubbed Clawdia's neck for a moment, then said, "You went all Willy Wonka on me."

I smiled. "I guess I did."

"You're serious about the store?"

"Absolutely. But there is one caveat."

"The name?"

I nodded. "You have to keep the name Bobbooks. It's my father's legacy."

Wendy smiled. "What happened, Noel? It's almost Dickensian, like you got visited by the ghosts of Christmas."

"Something like that. I learned the truth about my father."

"You learned that he was a good man?"

"I learned that he was a good *father*." As I looked at her, for the first time, I understood the depth of her pain. "I'm sorry that you couldn't be together."

"We *were* together. Every day. And that whole thing about getting married—I don't know if it would have worked, with Grace and everything."

"You had a love triangle going."

"Every good book does, right?"

"You know what's weird? You could have been my stepmother."

"That *would* have been weird."

"For the record, I never would have called you Mom."

"For the record, I wouldn't have let you." Clawdia suddenly jumped off Wendy's lap and ran out of the room. Wendy looked back at me. "Have you decided whether you're going back to New York?"

"I don't know. I guess it depends on my next visit."

"To Dylan's?"

I nodded.

"I hope it goes well for you."

"Thank you.

"If you decide to stay, we could always use you at the bookstore."

"I may take you up on that." I looked her in the eyes. "I'm going to finish my father's books."

She smiled. "You have no idea how much that would please him."

"I might."

"Would you like something to drink? I've got some wassail I could heat up. Coffee. Kombucha."

"Thank you, but I'd better go. Like I said, I've got one more stop to make."

As I stood up, Wendy walked over and hugged me. "I didn't get to be your stepmother, but, if it's okay, I'll be your sister."

My eyes welled. "I'd like that."

"I don't know how to thank you."

"You already have. You were there for my father when I wasn't. I'm very grateful for that. He deserved to be with someone who loved him."

She wiped her eyes. "It was hard. But I wouldn't trade a minute of our time together."

"You really did love him."

"With all my heart."

"So do I."

She sighed happily. "It's all he wanted." Her expression fell a little. "I'm really sorry about what I said to you at the store. Especially what I said about your dying alone. That was cruel."

"It was true. And I needed to hear it. Maybe you were my ghost of Christmas yet to come."

She smiled. "Maybe. Merry Christmas, Noel."

"You too, sister." I started to go, then turned back. "I have a strange question."

She cocked her head. "Yes?"

"Can butterflies live in winter?"

Her brow furrowed. "Butterflies? I think so. Why do you ask?"

"Just wondering." I kissed her cheek. "Merry Christmas, Wendy, and a Happy New Year."

CHAPTER

fifty–seven

One day I will find the right words, and they will be simple.

—Jack Kerouac

I drove back toward my home, exiting the highway on Highland Drive. Sugar House Park was full of life; myriad bright moving colors sliding down the hills. I had planned to go to Dylan's home, then thought better of it and, instead, drove to his parents' house. As I suspected, Dylan's truck was in the driveway.

I pulled up to the curb and parked. I got my bag of gifts, then walked to the front door and knocked.

Charlotte answered. She looked surprised to see me. "No-el."

"Merry Christmas, Charlotte."

"Merry Christmas to you, honey. Come on in."

"Thank you." After she shut the door, I handed her one of the presents. "This is for you."

"What is it?"

"Open it."

She tore off the wrapping. "A Jerica Bradley book. Thank you. I was going to get that one after the Christmas rush died down.

"Open the cover."

"The cover?" She opened the book. The title page was inscribed:

> Dear Charlotte,
> From one southern hen to another, Keep pecking.
> Jerica Bradley

She looked at me. "Jerica Bradley really wrote that?"

"Yes, she did," I said. "I have no idea what it means, but who else would write an inscription like that?"

"Thank you. I will treasure it."

"Is Dylan here?"

"He is. He's downstairs in the guest room taking a nap. Alex woke around four thirty. You know how kids are on Christmas morning. I'll go wake him."

"No. Please don't. I'll just go in, if you don't mind."

She looked at me for a moment, then said, "I think that will be okay."

"Are Stratton and Alex here?"

"They're in the den. It's down the hall."

I walked to the den. Alexis saw me as I walked in. "Noel!"

"Hi, sweetie."

"Daddy said I wouldn't get to see you anymore."

I frowned. "I would have missed you too much."

"Merry Christmas," Stratton said.

"Merry Christmas to you." I lifted my bag. "I brought presents."

"Do you have one for me?" Alexis asked.

I nodded. "Of course I do." I brought out her present. "You can probably tell it's a book. Do you like books?"

"Yes."

"Do you want to open it?"

"Uh-huh." She pulled back the wrapping paper to expose the children's book beneath.

"It's a book called *The Day the Crayons Came Home*," I said.

She laughed. "That's silly."

"I know. Maybe you and your grandpa can read it."

"I call him Pawpaw," she said.

"We'd love to," Stratton said.

"I have a present for you too," I said.

"You didn't need to do that. You caught me flat-footed. Now I'm in your debt."

"I'll always be in yours," I said. I handed him the wrapped book, which was as thick as a brick. "Dylan said you like non-fiction. I think you'll like it."

He pulled back the paper and held it up. *The Wright Brothers* by David McCullough.

"McCullough is a two-time Pulitzer Prize winner," I said.

"I'm familiar with McCullough. I read his book on Theodore Roosevelt."

"*Mornings on Horseback*," I said. "It won the National Book Award. My father loved it too."

"Thank you," he said. "It's a very fine gift."

"I'm glad you like it."

He set the book down. "More than that, I'm glad you came. Dylan's been pining for you. I hate seeing that."

"I'm sorry," I said softly. "I didn't treat him like he deserved to be treated." I shook my head. "I haven't really been the person I want to be."

Stratton smiled at me kindly. "Well, I suppose admitting that is the first step to becoming that person."

"Thank you," I said.

"Merry Christmas, Noel."

"Merry Christmas, Mr. Sparks."

"Pawpaw, can you read this to me?" Alexis said, holding up her book.

"How about you read it to me?"

"Okay."

Stratton winked at me. "Dylan's in the guest room. It's the first door down the stairs."

"Thank you."

I was afraid to see him. I wouldn't be surprised if he made me leave. I guess I expected it. I wouldn't blame him, either.

I softly walked down the carpeted stairs and opened the door. Dylan was asleep, snoring a little. I gently sat on the bed and then lay back, my face next to his. For several minutes I just watched him sleep. He was beautiful. My mind and heart both raced. I had no idea what I would say to him when he woke. My anxiety grew. Why wouldn't he throw me out? I was considering leaving when his eyes fluttered open. He looked as surprised as I thought he would. His voice was raspy as he said, "I thought you were Alex."

"I'm sorry. It's just me."

"I'm not used to waking up to a strange woman in bed."

"That's probably good."

He smiled slightly.

My eyes were locked on his. "Do you think you could get used to it?"

"Maybe. With a little practice."

"I would love to practice waking up with you."

He just looked at me. My eyes welled up. "I'm so sorry, Dylan. You've been nothing but good to me." I swallowed. "Everything you said about me was true. You have no reason to forgive me. But if you could somehow give me another chance . . ." I closed my eyes as tears rolled down my cheeks. "I'll be better. I promise. I—"

I didn't finish, as he pressed his lips against mine. I fell back onto the bed as we kissed. After a while he leaned back and looked into my eyes. "Apology accepted."

"I'm not done."

"You have more to say? You kind of said a lot already."

I smiled. "I meant with the kissing part."

E P I L O G U E

This might be the happy ending without the ending.
—David Levithan

TWO YEARS LATER

I settled myself in at the small round table near the back of Bobbooks while Dylan brought over a cup of coffee.

"So, how does this thing work?" he asked, handing me the mug.

"Thank you, honey," I said as he sat down. "You just take their books and open it to the Post-it Note, if there is one. If they have more than one book, you can stack them inside each other."

"Like taco shells."

I smiled. "Just like taco shells."

While Cammy, Cyndee, and a new girl, Lark, sold books, Alex and Teddy walked up and down my line handing out Post-it Notes so my readers could write down who they wanted me to sign their book to.

Wendy walked up behind us. "I wish your father was here to see this."

"I'm pretty sure he is," I said.

"Of course he is," Grace said.

It was no surprise that Grace was first in line, especially since the book was dedicated to her. I had invited her as my special guest, and we let her in early through the employees' entrance.

Wendy smiled at me. "Are you ready?"

"I think she's thirty-years ready," Dylan said. "Let's get this show on the road."

"Good," Wendy said. "Thank you for having your first signing here."

"You know my dad would kill me if I didn't. Thank you for having me."

Teddy walked up to me with Alexis by his side. She was nine now, and nearly as outspoken as I had been at her age. "Dude, your line goes down the block."

"She's not a dude," Alexis said. "She's a lady."

"My apologies. So, before the mayhem commences, may I get your autograph? It's like you're a celebrity now."

"She's not a celebrity," Alexis said. "She's my mom."

"Dude, celebrity, it's all good," I said. I took one of my books from the table and signed it. "There you go, Teddy. It's my gift."

"Thanks. I promise I won't sell it on eBay."

"You can do whatever you want with it. It's yours."

Alex was right, by the way. Dylan and I married just six months after that Christmas. Dylan already had the wedding tuxedos, and Wendy let us hold the ceremony at the bookstore. It was perfect. At least perfectly us. Wendy was my maid of honor. Grace arranged for our wedding cake. It was gorgeous and was made to look like a stack of books, with the names of the books written in frosting. I'm sure my father would have loved every bit of it.

I never went back to New York. I worked remotely with Jerica on a couple more of her books (yes, I won the battle and she learned to email me her manuscripts) but finally decided it wasn't worth the aggravation. She was surprisingly gracious when I told her that I was quitting to work on my own book. She even gave me a blurb for the jacket.

After our wedding, I moved in with Dylan. Wendy sold her home and purchased mine to be closer to the store, though I don't really think that was her prime motivation. I'm happy to report that Bobbooks now has a café. Teddy is the chief barista. He was perfect for the job, as he had worked at a Starbucks for two years before coming to us.

The café part was Wendy's choice, of course. She said, "Robert will probably let me have it in the next life, but it's worth it for now." It has added a nice cushion to her bottom line. Business is good, and she's now looking at expanding into the space next door. She's even thought of opening a second store.

On a more personal note, Wendy's dating someone now. He's cute, and he's younger than she is. And he goes by Bobby. I'm just glad she's not alone.

Dylan and I are looking at a little expansion ourselves. I'm five months pregnant. So far so good. Alexis is hoping for a little sister. I totally get that.

In addition to the café, Wendy's done a little more remodeling. She put a little plaque up on the wall near the entrance with a picture of my father. Engraved in brass are these words by Vonnegut:

A purpose of human life, no matter who is controlling it, is to love whoever is around to be loved.

Life is good. For my wedding present, Wendy had my father's letters bound into a book with the title *Tabula Rasa: Love Letters from a Father to His Daughter*.

I have reread the letters many times now. Someday I'll pass the book on to my own children. I like the concept of a tabula rasa. There is a time in all our lives that we need to clear the slate, trusting that the truth will set us free. For many, freedom is terrifying. I understand. It's not always easy and it never feels safe, but truth is always worth the risk. Always.

Interestingly enough, I've even learned something about butterflies. In some cultures, butterflies are believed to be visitations from a deceased loved one. They are also a sign to leave our pasts behind.

Every now and then I'll be reading a book and I'll look up and there will be a butterfly. Maybe it's magical thinking. Maybe it's just selective attention. Then again, maybe it isn't. Just in case, I always smile and say, "I miss you too, Dad."

I really do.

ACKNOWLEDGMENTS

I wish to acknowledge the life and impact of Carolyn Reidy. In 1995, Carolyn brought me into the Simon & Schuster family and has, until this book, been with me for the entire ride. I'm grateful for her faith in me, her professionalism, and her wisdom. I will miss you, Carolyn.

I'm grateful for Jonathan Karp, who has stepped into Carolyn's large shoes. He, too, has been a solid companion and welcome sojourner in my literary career. Thank you, Jon.

Thanks to my new Gallery family: Jennifer Bergstrom, Aimée Bell, Jennifer Long, and the rest of the Gallery crew. Thank you for the home and the attention to my books. With this book I welcome a new editor, Hannah Braaten. Thank you for your help, Hannah. Thank you for enduring the slings and arrows of outrageous deadlines so I could focus on writing. Don't say I didn't warn you.

Laurie Liss. Dear agent, we have yet again dodged a bullet.

My assistant, Diane Glad. Thanks for the lemonade. Eleven years and counting.

My wife, Keri. Thank you for being you. I love you and I always will.

ABOUT THE AUTHOR

Richard Paul Evans is the #1 bestselling author of *The Christmas Box* and the Michael Vey series. Each of his more than thirty-five novels has been a *New York Times* bestseller. There are more than thirty-five million copies of his books in print worldwide, translated into more than twenty-four languages. He is the recipient of numerous awards, including the American Mothers Book Award, the Romantic Times Best Women's Novel of the Year Award, the German Audience Gold Award for Romance, five Religion Communicators Council Wilbur Awards, the Washington Times Humanitarian of the Century Award, and the Volunteers of America Empathy Award. He lives in Salt Lake City, Utah, with his wife, Keri, not far from their five children and two grandchildren. You can learn more about Richard on Facebook at www.facebook.com/RPEfans or read his blog at www.richardpaulevans.com.

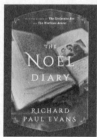
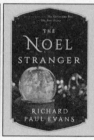
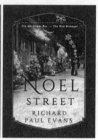

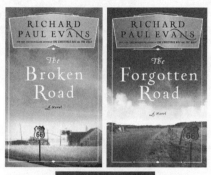